DON'T STOP BEWITCHING

A Happily Everlasting Series World Novel

MANDY M. ROTH

Don't Stop Bewitching © Copyright 2018 by Mandy M. Roth

ALL RIGHTS RESERVED.

All books copyrighted to the author and may not be resold or given away without written permission from the author, Mandy M. Roth.

This novel is a work of fiction. Any and all characters, events, and places are of the author's imagination and should not be confused with fact. Any resemblance to persons, living or dead, or events or places is merely coincidence. Novel intended for adults only. Must be 18 years or older to read.

Published by Raven Happy Hour LLC
www.RavenHappyHour.com
Raven Books and all affiliate sites and projects are © Copyrighted 2004-2018

Featured Titles from Mandy M. Roth

The Immortal Ops Series World
Immortal Ops
Critical Intelligence
Radar Deception
Strategic Vulnerability
Tactical Magik
Act of Mercy
Administrative Control
Act of Surrender
Broken Communication
Separation Zone
Act of Submission
Damage Report
Act of Command
Wolf's Surrender

The Dragon Shifter's Duty
Midnight Echoes
Isolated Maneuver
Expecting Darkness
Area of Influence
Act of Passion
Act of Brotherhood
Healing the Wolf
Wrecked Intel
And more to come…

Cozy Paranormal Mysteries
Once Hunted, Twice Shy
Total Eclipse of the Hunt
And more to come…

Tempting Fate Series
Loup Garou
Bad Moon Rising
And more to come…

The Guardians Series
The Guardians
Crossing Hudson
Ruling Jude
And more to come…

The Druid Series
Sacred Places
Goddess of the Grove
Winter Solstice
A Druid of Her Own
And more to come…

The King of Prey Series
King of Prey
A View to a Kill
Master of the Hunt
Rise of the King
Prince of Pleasure
Prince of Flight

Bureau of Paranormal Investigation (BPI)
Hunted Holiday
Heated Holiday
And more to come…

FAQs

Q: What other characters will Mandy be writing about from the Everlasting/ Bewitchingly Ever After worlds?
A: The ones she created: Leo, Sigmund, Petey, Wilber, Jolene, the devil, York, Louis, Blackbeard, etc. These books will be part of Mandy's spin-off series from Happily Everlasting--Bewitchingly Ever After.

Q: Will Mandy write other cozies that are not part of the Everlasting world?
A: Yes. She's working on a few series right now and will notify her mailing list when more information becomes available.

FAQs

Q: What series are related to Bewitchingly Ever After?
A: The Happily Everlasting Series

Blurb

Don't Stop Bewitching: A Happily Everlasting Series World Novel (Bewitchingly Ever After)
by
Mandy M. Roth

Welcome to Hedgewitch Cove, Louisiana, where there's no such thing as normal.

town

Cat-shifter Curt Warrick doesn't want to take a road trip with five other guys but when his best friend leaves him no choice, he finds himself in a van, stuffed full of men, headed to Louisiana. It should come as no surprise when everything that could go wrong on the trip does. That's okay though, Curt is used to the weird and wacky, after all, he was born and raised in a town that is the epitome of it all. There is a bright side. The trip will give him a chance to expand his enterprise.

There is nothing Missi (Mississippi) Peugeot hates more than rich men who think they can throw money around to get what they want. Okay, that's a lie. She hates change. That's why she's happy to stay in her tiny hometown of Hedgewitch Cove, Louisiana. Protected by magic, the town has kept its quaint, cozy feel—that is until a flashy, yet fetching, stranger shows up in a van that screams "flower power," announcing he's looking to buy property and begin developing the town. Missi's grandmother always warned her that her words had consequences. When she speaks out of anger, the magic in her rises to the challenge, putting a curse on Curt. Not that the man needed any help in the cursed department, seeing as how he already has a spell of chaos cast over him. By who, they don't know.

Now Missi just has to keep Mr. Flashy alive long enough to get him back up north where he belongs before her words come back to haunt him. There is only one slight hiccup with her plan: every second she tries to keep mishap from befalling Curt leaves her one step closer to wanting him to stay.

Chapter One

CURT WARRICK STOOD next to his best friend since childhood, staring at the brightly colored monstrosity before them. They'd been doing so for the greater part of fifteen minutes, as they ignored the heat this time of year, each trying to soak in what they were looking at. While Curt understood it was a Volkswagen van, his mind was having a hard time wrapping itself around the idea that anyone would ever get in it, let alone pick it for a long road trip. Yet there it was, parked on Main Street, in front of Hunted Treasures Antiques & Artifacts Shop. "I'm not sure it's road worthy."

Hugh Lupine, Curt's best friend and

fellow shifter, crossed his arms over his chest. "I'm *positive* it's not road worthy. No way are we getting in that. It's a death trap. I'm not biting the big one by way of flower power. I've got a baby due soon. I plan to be alive for its arrival. I changed my mind about the charter jet. Make the call, Warrick."

"Your wish is my command." Nodding, Curt withdrew his cell phone from his back pocket and ignored the sweat beading on his spine from the heat. As a shifter male, his core body temperature ran hotter than a human's. The addition of humid summer weather didn't help matters any.

Curt dropped his phone before he actually made any call or booked anything, and the phone just missed landing in a puddle, left over from the storms that had passed through overnight. With a groan, he retrieved it.

He'd done very well for himself and invested wisely. Having a private jet ready for them to depart on within the next two hours wasn't a hardship by any means. He'd done so numerous times before. When he'd learned of some prime commercial property that might be up for grabs in the town where they were headed to, he'd looked into and had nearly booked a jet then and there. He was now regretting his choice to wait.

"Don't book a plane, Curt. It will be fun for you guys to have a road trip. It will give you so many great memories together. Plus, when you get down there, you can check on Sig and see how he's doing. And I think the van is pretty," said Penelope, Hugh's wife.

She was wearing a pair of leggings with small wolf heads all over them, a bright blue maternity shirt with the same wolf-head print all over it, and a hat (that was for winter but it was hotter than heck out) that looked like someone knitted wolf ears on it with a pair of dangly earrings that were little red and white lighthouses. Curt wasn't so sure they should let her have a vote on anything, let alone the vehicle that would need to take them over a thousand miles.

When Penelope's paternal grandfather, Wilber Messing, announced he needed to travel to Hedgewitch Cove, Louisiana, to deliver a special package (which totally meant supernatural artifacts), one that couldn't be sent by normal means, Penelope and her new best friend Kelsey had gotten it in their heads that the trip should include a number of men. Not just Wilber. The girls firmly believed it would be a manly road trip, full of fun and comradery.

It was as if the women didn't know a single one of the men they'd wrangled into going.

The varying personalities they'd assembled would clash within a mile from town. If that. Making it over a thousand miles together would never work. They'd be lucky to make it down Main Street before someone ended up killing someone else. Curt's money was on Wilber killing Hugh. Wilber might have been up there in years, but the man was a natural-born hunter and spry. It was in his blood to eliminate supernaturals.

Curt hoped that was true or they'd all be listed as missing persons very soon.

Showing up in Hedgewitch Cove minus a few passengers was a real concern when everyone involved in the road trip was either a card-carrying member of the supernatural club or a born hunter. The two were already oil and water. Hunters weren't technically classified as supernaturals even though they were. They'd refused to allow themselves to be listed in the books on the paranormal as supernaturals. They were elitists who fancied themselves a cut above all those they were born to police and, like their name suggested, hunt.

They'd had a number of names over the centuries—slayers, hunters, exorcists, etc. Under it all they were a bunch of people who looked down their noses at the supernatural. Depending on the hunter, they might or might not simply kill every supernatural they encountered.

Hunters had been known for doing just that.

Wilber swore he'd turned over a new leaf after the death of his son, Penelope's father, at the hands of hunters who didn't much care for the fact that Penelope's mother had befriended supernaturals and championed their cause.

Curt could only hope Wilber was telling

the truth about his killing days being long behind him. Especially if they were all riding in the same van from Maine to Louisiana. Curt had never been to Hedgewitch Cove before and knew very little about the town, other than it was like Everlasting—a safe haven for supernaturals. He'd been told it was just outside of New Orleans and he'd been there plenty of times. There was always a good time to be had in the French Quarter. He just wasn't so sure getting there would be very fun. Not with his travel buddies.

So far, Penelope and Kelsey had managed to rope Curt, Hugh, Wilber, Jake, and Leo in their boys-trip plan. None of the men were willing participants. That didn't seem to matter much to the women.

The only one of the group the women hadn't asked was Petey Williams. The yet-to-be-determined-crazy older wolf-shifter had just declared himself part of the gang and then informed everyone that he had the perfect ride. Which led to their current predicament.

Petey's perfect ride was more like a

perfect nightmare. The van was held together by peace sign stickers, painted flowers, dirt, rust, and the will of the gods (not necessarily in that order). A strong wind could take it out. That or a car wash, maybe even just a heavy rain. It was a moving eyesore and didn't look safe to drive or ride in.

"She's cherry, isn't she?" asked the older man, grinning from ear to ear. His eyes twinkled with merriment and it was easy to see Petey truly thought he was contributing to the trip. It was hard to be annoyed with him. His help always came from a good place, despite it more often than not leaving nothing but chaos in its wake.

His salt-and-pepper hair poked out from under his black knit cap that he was rarely without regardless the time of year. He was in a gray T-shirt with holes in it, that had a logo for his bait and tackle shop and a pair of yellow rain pants over his jeans. He had better clothing. Both Curt and Hugh always made sure the man had whatever he needed. The problem with Petey was, he didn't need much. He liked living simply and wasn't materialistic in the least. Petey was an old-school fisherman and it showed, from the weathered lines on his face and his permanently tanned skin to the fishing boots he seemed to always be in.

That being said, the guy would do anything for anyone. He had that big of a heart.

Curt didn't relish the thought of hurting the man's feelings, but he disliked the idea even more that his end would come within the hippie van. Supernatural didn't mean he couldn't die. It just meant he was harder to kill.

"Petey, I don't know about this," said Curt, wanting to soften the blow.

Hugh cast the fisherman a sideways glance. "This thing is a rolling piece of strawberry shortcake."

Curt snorted. Hugh wasn't one to pull punches.

The wolf-shifter had been subjected to a potion that left him saying off-the-wall things in place of curse words. That had been back in October and Hugh had gone from being able to weave a string of curses together that would shock anyone, to calling people baked goods and other silly names. His mate preferred that to Hugh's foul mouth, so Hugh stuck with it, even after the potion had worn off. That was a testament to just how much Hugh loved his wife, Penelope.

Hugh came in at six and a half feet tall (an inch taller than Curt) and was hardly a small guy. He also leaked alpha male as he walked.

Curt snickered. "Strawberry shortcake. Ooo, hardcore. What's next? Peach cobbler?"

Hugh shoved him, making Curt lose his balance. His best friend grabbed him and steadied him before pulling him into a manly hug.

Hugh was not a hugger.

The man was as far from a hugger as you could get.

Yet, he held Curt to him in a tight embrace.

Curt's eyes widened as he stood clamped against the wolf-shifter. "Uh, Hugh? You been hitting Petey's stash?"

Petey snorted. "He always throws away my good stuff, so I hide it."

Hugh stepped back fast, held out his arms, and stared at them as if they weren't attached to him and weren't his own. "What the blueberry pancakes was that about? *They* just hugged you."

"They?" echoed Curt.

Hugh nodded, appearing stunned. "It wasn't me. I didn't do that."

"Yes, you did. I was on the other end of the hug. Trust me, it was you. Also, I'd like it noted that your new aftershave smells nice."

Hugh's nostrils flared. "I did not hug you. My arms did."

"That made less sense than your baking curses," said Curt.

Hugh grunted. "But it's true."

Curt watched his friend. "Dude, admit it. You're into me. I'm alluring like that. It's why you wore the new aftershave, isn't it? You wanted me to notice you."

With a growl, Hugh narrowed his gaze on Curt. "Warrick, don't make me eat you."

"You could try. You forget, I'm a lion-shifter. I'm capable of giving as good as I get. Don't let the designer clothing fool you. I can throw down with the best of them," said Curt with a wink. While he tended to joke off nearly everything, his words were not a lie. He was a powerful lion-shifter, born from a line of pure-bloods. While he was as alpha as Hugh, he didn't walk around wearing it on his sleeve for all to see. There was no need to. But should the need ever arise, he'd accept the challenge. "Want to hug some more?"

"I'm going to throttle you!" Hugh's arms flew out again, this time looking like he really wasn't in control of them. "What the…?"

Petey hooked his thumbs behind his white and blue polka dot suspenders, which were currently holding up his bright yellow rain pants. "I knew you wouldn't be able to resist the peanut butter cookies I left out on your kitchen table. You've always had a sweet tooth, Lupine."

Hugh paled, his arms still held out wide, as if he was waiting for an embrace. "Tell me you didn't slip a Polly potion in something I ate."

Curt failed to hide his laugh. The only thing that would have made the moment better was if their other best friend, Sigmund Bails, were present to witness it. As it stood, Sig was down in Hedgewitch Cove—their destination.

Hugh had already fallen victim to potions in baked goods and drinks more than once. Aunt Polly, a witch with a big heart and a colorful approach to life, seemed to take great pleasure in using the wolf as a test subject. He'd once gotten fleas from one of her potions. She'd also been the one behind the potion that had left Hugh saying cute things in place of curse words for the month of October. It had been Polly's way of assuring she won the pool the town had going.

Had Polly not taken matters into her own hands, Hugh would have lost the friendly wager he and Curt had going. As it stood, Hugh won with flying colors, not to mention flying baked good rants. It had given Curt so much amusement that it had been worth losing the bet and having to donate five thousand dollars to the middle school fund. Besides, the money had gone to a good cause, so it was worth it in the end.

Apparently, Curt was in for more fun at Hugh's expense. That was really the best kind of fun to be had. A long road trip in a van from hippie-hell was totally worth it.

"You slipped me more Polly potion?" asked Hugh, shock and horror reflected on his face.

Petey whistled low and did his best to appear as if he wasn't the guilty party. "Not exactly. She's out in Lucky Valley, you know. Well, some folks call it *Unlucky* Valley, but I suppose that's neither here nor there." He bit his lower lip slightly. "We sort of had to make our own potion this time. It's to help your temperament for the long road trip. It's supposed to make you feel love and happiness and all the stuff opposite how you'd normally feel on a road trip with the guys. Tried some myself first just to be sure it wouldn't kill you. Works like a charm. Made me so happy I couldn't stop singing for two days."

Curt laughed so hard he teared up. "That explains the forty-eight hours' worth of songs from the *Wizard of Oz* soundtrack you subjected us all to the other day down at the marina."

Petey smiled wider. "Penelope got me the soundtrack from the Broadway show *Wicked*. Wait until you hear my rendition of 'Defying Gravity.'"

"Did you know about this?" demanded Hugh as he faced his wife.

Penelope smiled and then hugged him. "Of course I did. I baked the cookies, remember? I'm happy it worked. Kelsey and I weren't so sure it would since we mixed the potion ourselves. Sure, we had a list of ingredients to go off of, but Aunt Polly's penmanship left a little something to be desired. And since she's out of town, we couldn't ask her about it. Looks like we were right to go with the *dried bat wing* and not the *dirty bath water*, Petey. Good call."

"When you weren't looking, I put some of my leftover bathwater in the mix just in case the recipe said that and not bat wings. Figured it was best to cover all our bases." Petey waggled his bushy brows. "And to be extra sure it worked, I used the same water to bathe in all last week. It was good and dirty. No room for error."

Curt scrunched up his face in disgust, happy he hadn't given in to the temptation of eating one of the cookies. They'd looked delicious when he'd been in Hugh's house earlier.

"To be clear," said Hugh, grunting as he finally got his arms lowered. They shot back up again, and it was evident he was not pleased. "My wife, her friend, and a guy I see as a father figure decided to possibly poison me to make me nicer on a road trip? And now I can't control the urge to hug people?"

Penelope and Petey shared a look before nodding.

"Yes," said Penelope, hugging her husband more. "That's exactly what we did. But like Petey said, he tested it first so it's hardly fair to call it poisoning you. He lived.

He hasn't been any more huggy than normal. That is a *you* thing."

"You're not the best traveler," added Petey, tugging at his suspenders more. "There was that time on the train when you wanted to eat the conductor. Then the other time when you took me to the Big Apple and you really did try to eat the cab driver."

Curt remembered the day well. He, Sigmund, Hugh, and Petey had gone to New York City and one of the cab drivers had been a were-bird. The man would not stop taunting Hugh, clearly not a fan of wolf-shifters. It took both Curt and Sig to pull their friend away from the cab driver before any real damage could be done. Petey had threatened to defeather the man but had let the matter drop when told to.

Hugh got his arms down and they stayed that way. He then lifted each one slowly and wiggled his fingers as if he wasn't sure he was in full control once more.

Petey continued. "And then there was

that time we were driving down to Florida with Buster and you—"

Hugh put up a hand, stopping Petey. "I get it. Fine. I'm not the best traveler."

"Not the best?" questioned Penelope. "Sweetie, you're difficult on most days. From what I've been told you're nearly impossible to deal with on road trips. Grandpa promised to be on his best behavior and this will ensure you are too."

Hugh grunted. "I told you I would be."

"And five minutes later you were goading Grandpa," she reminded him.

Curt had been there during it all and already knew Wilber and Hugh couldn't be together more than five minutes before one was at the other.

Penelope sighed. "I love you both. I want you to learn to get along. The constant bickering has gone on too long. You're going to be a father before you know it. It's time you start acting like an adult. This will help."

"Did you make Wilber eat Petey's dirty bathwater too?" asked Hugh, sounding a lot more like a child than a grown alpha male.

None of it boded well in the making-him-an-adult angle.

Penelope bit her lower lip and blushed. "We tried, but Grandpa didn't fall for the cookies. You did."

Curt bent, laughing too hard to bother hiding it. When he reached the point of snorting, Hugh cuffed him on the back of the ear. Standing straight, Curt glanced at Penelope. "I think he needs another cookie."

Hugh growled.

Curt merely laughed more and dodged another cuff to the ear. "Hey, it could have been worse."

"How so?"

"You could be singing about heading off the see the wizard while trying to hug me." Curt grinned. "You'd look great in a tutu as part of the Lollipop Guild."

Hugh tipped his head. "You're thinking of the Lullaby League."

Curt wiped his hand over his mouth and snorted. "The fact you know the difference is very telling."

"My mate likes the movie and has made

me sit through it more than once in the last few months," said Hugh.

Curt nodded. "Sure she has."

"Please note the cookie didn't take my urge to end you," warned Hugh with a very wolfish growl.

Penelope pushed on the man's chest. "Stop. You'd never really hurt him. You love him like a brother."

"Want me to write a song about it?" asked Petey, grinning wide. "I've been working on some original material. You could express your love for Curt in a ballad, or I could do something you could dance ballet to since you're into that and all."

Curt couldn't breathe as he laughed even harder.

"I am not into…never mind." Hugh looked at Curt and grinned mischievously. "Hey, Warrick. How about a friendly wager?"

Penelope groaned. "Not again."

Petey rocked more on the balls of his feet. "The last one ended well for Hugh. He won, plus he got himself a wife and a little one on the way. Maybe Curt will win this one and get himself a family too. You know matings normally happen in groupings. If I was younger, I'd be worried it was gonna happen to me."

Curt moved back so fast that he tripped over his own two feet and would have fallen had someone not caught his arm and yanked him upright. He glanced up to find Deputy Jake Majoy standing there, a puzzled look on the man's face. He had on a black jacket with the word "Sheriff" written across the front breast pocket in bright yellow. The centaur had been born to help police supernaturals. It was in his blood. So much so he apparently dressed the part even when not on duty.

"You look like you're going to be sick, Warrick," said Jake before handing Curt something. "Here. You dropped this."

Curt stared down into Jake's hand at a half-dollar-sized gold coin with a lion's head on it. "That's not mine."

Jake stared at him. "Uh, yeah it is. I think it fell out of your pocket just now when you were looking as if you might run or pass out."

Petey chortled. "Talk of mating freaks the boy out."

Curt took the coin from Jake's hand and studied it a moment before shrugging. "This isn't mine."

"We could argue about it all day, but I'm telling you, it fell out of your pocket," said Jake.

Curt slid the coin into his front pocket and let the matter drop. He'd give the gold piece to Wilber later. It was probably one of the man's antiques that had found its way out and to the ground in front of his shop.

"This is so exciting. The boys will have a ton of fun," said Jake's wife, Kelsey. She was next to him, one hand on her swollen stomach, smiling as she gave Penelope a wave.

"Boys?" questioned Jake.

Kelsey patted her husband's arm. "Yes. *Boys*. I've seen you all in action before. Remember?"

Petey went straight for Kelsey and hugged her.

She returned the embrace. "Are you all set for the trip?"

"I am. Got Sunshine. She's something.

A true beauty." Petey thumbed towards the van.

Kelsey looked at it and clapped with excitement. "I love it! She's everything you said she was."

"And more," added Curt in a hushed tone, earning him nods from Hugh and Jake. "Jake, ask Hugh about his love of tutus, but be mindful of random bouts of hugging."

"Don't make me shove my sunflower up your whoops-a-daisy," said Hugh as his arms shot out again. His jaw set in frustration. He sent a scathing look in Petey's direction.

The older man didn't seem to mind in the least.

Kelsey laughed. "It worked! Yay! We did it."

She high-fived Penelope.

Jake stared around at the group. "Did what? And why does Hugh look like he wants to hug Warrick?"

"They poisoned me," returned Hugh.

Penelope grunted. "Did not."

"You fed me Petey's dirty bathwater,"

argued Hugh. "That qualifies as poisoning me."

Jake rubbed his temple. "Just when I think this town couldn't possibly get any weirder."

"Nah," said Petey with a shake of his head. "Everlasting isn't that bad. We're going to Hedgewitch Cove. I used to live there. It's way weirder than this. In fact, it makes Everlasting look downright normal."

"You lived in Hedgewitch Cove?" asked Hugh, surprise in his voice. "How did I not know this?"

Curt hadn't known that fact either.

"Oh yes. Petey was there for its start. Lived there for a decent amount of time." Kelsey looped her arm through Petey's. The two had become close quickly. Kelsey had arrived in Everlasting around a month after Penelope and the two had connected instantly, both bonding quickly with the old fisherman.

Kelsey and Petey had a special relationship. He took on a very protective, fatherly role with her. Kelsey seemed happy with it all and filled a void the older gentleman had.

Petey touched Kelsey's swollen stomach and bent, putting his mouth near the woman's stomach. "How are you doing today, little one?"

Kelsey rubbed her lower back. "Active. I feel like the baby is running a marathon nonstop in there."

Jake grinned and kissed his wife's cheek. "I should stay home. What if you need me?"

"I'll be fine," said Kelsey, giving him a stern look.

Petey laughed. "She's sick of you hovering. Same as Penelope with Hugh."

"My wife could go into labor any minute," said Hugh. "I'm staying."

Penelope pointed at him. "You already tried that one. Dr. Prescott already told you that it's more than common for hunter pregnancies to be slightly longer than a normal supernatural's and the baby is showing no signs of coming soon."

Kelsey put her hand out to Penelope

and the two moved closer together. "I, for one, need a break from the men."

"Totally," said Penelope with a smile. "Mine is nesting."

"He's what?" asked Curt, wondering what in the world his best friend had in common with a bird.

Petey whistled and shook his head. "The boy already has the nursery all fixed up and ready to go. He's babyproofed the entire house to the point Penelope is ready to poison him for real. Took her thirty minutes to get into the refrigerator for a snack the other day. If there is one thing you do not do, it's come between a pregnant woman and food."

Hugh slumped his shoulders. "I took the child lock off the top of the fridge. Can I *please* stay home? I'll behave myself. I promise."

Curt snorted. "Remember when you used to be alpha?"

Hugh lunged, and Curt dodged his friend's attempt at getting him.

Curt stepped back and tossed his hands

up. "Stop. I don't want to be hugged again."

Hugh groaned.

The women laughed.

Curt glanced at Jake. "Excited to have some male bonding time with your brother-in-law?"

Jake wasn't quick enough to school his expression. From the look of it, the last thing he wanted to do was spend time with Kelsey's brother, Leo, who was apparently running late. Leo had been working on the docks for the last few months, keeping to himself mostly, but lingering around town, no doubt to be close to his sister.

While Leo and Jake didn't see eye to eye, he and Wilber seemed to get along just fine. It didn't surprise Curt that Leo and Wilber had hit it off. Probably had something to do with the fact they were both hunters. Though Leo's line of hunters had magic as well.

All that meant was they were better at standing against supernaturals.

That didn't give Curt any warm or

fuzzy feelings considering he, himself, was a supernatural.

Hugh faced Petey. "How is it Kelsey knows you lived in Hedgewitch Cove and I don't? I've known you all my life. You practically live with me."

"She's a better listener," said Petey before taking Kelsey's hand and dragging her in the direction of the van. He began pointing out various painted flowers.

Jake eyed Petey. "When Kelsey told me you spent time there, I was shocked. No wonder you were *all* for me taking Sigmund there to help learn to control his shifter side."

At the mention of Sigmund, Curt smiled. He, Sig, and Hugh had basically been best friends since birth. Having Sigmund gone for months had been hard and odd. Curt had been used to popping over to Sig's house to hang out with him at random and used to having an ally against Hugh and his temper. Sig was always the voice of reason. Always the peacemaker amongst the group of friends. Before his entire world had turned upside down when he came into his supernatural gifts, Sig had been a pacifist.

All that had changed seemingly overnight.

Sig had come into his shifting abilities recently, when most males did so in their teens. His were-kraken side had gotten away from him, and in the end, two bad guys were left dead. Sig's guilt nearly ate him alive. He not only needed guidance on how to control his newly found shifter side, he needed time to heal mentally as well and to come to grips with the fact he'd done what needed to be done.

When Jake had first taken Sig to Louisiana, it was with the understanding Sig would be gone a month or so. That was eight months ago, and the man was showing no signs of returning.

The rare moments Curt spoke to his friend on the phone, Sig was vague about returning. It was to the point that Curt wasn't sure Sig ever planned to return to Everlasting. That wasn't okay with Curt.

Sig was part of Everlasting.

He belonged here.

Jake checked his phone before glancing up at Petey. "You could have told me you used to live in Hedgewitch Cove. I'd have had you ride down with me when I took Sig there."

Petey shrugged and rubbed his chin. "Wasn't the right time for me to go back just then. Polly and me sat down and had a little talk. She let me know the stars were aligned and that the time is now. Guess I gotta face my past at some point. No time like the present. You ever call that realtor I told you about?"

"I did." Curt nodded. "It's worth checking out the property he mentioned might be available. It's not far from the waterfront either. The price range he gave me was low."

"Is it a toxic waste facility?" asked Hugh.

"No. Well, I'm not sure. It's close to a magic shop so one can never be too sure," said Curt. Petey had shown him an old listing online that talked about the property. Since Curt was always looking for ways to diversify his income, and he was already quite successful in the restaurant business, it seemed wise to at least look at the property if they were heading there anyway. "Can't hurt to check it out while I'm there. I'm planning to toss Sig in the trunk and bring him back home with us too, so there is that. We should get a move on it. We're burning daylight."

"You don't want to get in that van any more than I do. Now you're pushing for quality guy time?" questioned Hugh.

Penelope leaned against him. "He's right. And I know you know it. You're thinking the same thing as Curt, but he's man enough to admit it out loud."

Curt grinned. "Hear that? I'm manly. I told you cat-shifters were the dominant species."

"Yeah, right." Jake shoved him playfully and then picked up a leather backpack and carried it towards the van. "All right, folks, are we doing this? Curt is right. We're wasting daylight."

Hugh pointed to Jake's bag. "Warrick, see that. He only has one small bag too. Unlike you, prima donna, who needed two large ones. Is one full of your hair products?"

Curt adjusted the collar of his shirt and waggled his brows. "Yes. The ladies like a man who takes pride in his appearance."

Petey took off his knit cap, licked his palm, and then ran it through his hair. "It's true. Ladies love us well-kept men."

Penelope laughed and came at Curt to hug him. A second before she got to him, she launched into a fit of sneezes, reminding everyone that she was allergic to cats. It was something Hugh got great joy from since it meant she was basically allergic to Curt.

Curt wrapped his arms around her. "I'll keep him out of trouble."

"Thank you," she said, kissing his cheek chastely.

"Don't be hanging on my wife," said Hugh, his voice teasing.

Curt smiled. "Pretty sure you staked your territory there. You claimed her and she's about to pop with your little one."

"Pop?" asked Penelope. "Are you saying I'm big?"

Curt stiffened. "No. I'd never say that. You're stunning. In fact, pregnancy suits you. You're even more beautiful as an expectant mother. You glow."

She snorted. "Smooth talker."

Hugh grumbled. "If he keeps smooth talking you, I'm going to…"

Curt flashed a smile. "You're going to what? Hug me some more? Call me a baked good? Threaten me with flowers?"

Hugh made a move to come at Curt.

Penelope stepped between them. "Boys."

They sighed.

Jake snorted.

Kelsey gave him a hard look.

He lowered his gaze.

"That's what I thought," said Kelsey as she moved away from them quickly, in the direction of Jake's SUV.

"Baby, what are you doing? I don't get a kiss good-bye?" asked Jake of Kelsey.

"I'm not going yet." She stepped off the edge of the sidewalk and wobbled as she lost her footing. Curt and Jake took off behind her, each reaching for her to make sure she didn't fall.

Jake nodded a thank you at Curt before staying by his mate's side as she opened the back door of his SUV. She pulled out a picnic basket and a large thermos.

"I almost forgot this stuff." She glanced down at her stomach. "My center of gravity is way off now. I trip over my own two feet all the time."

Jake eased the basket from her hands and dipped his head, giving his wife a tender kiss. "Mmm, thanks, baby. But do me a favor and be extra careful. I love you and you're carrying precious cargo."

She grinned. "Are you planning to tell me if our baby will be born able to shift partly into a horse or are you still pleading the fifth on that one, Mr. Centaur?"

"Fifth," said Jake with a grin. "I'm going to miss you. I don't want to be gone from you."

"Jake, I know the only reason you haven't babyproofed the house yet is because you heard Penelope and me making fun of Hugh for going overboard. You're just as bad as him. I know you're excited about being a father but, honey, you're driving me ten kinds of crazy. I want to relax and not have you running around the house, worrying over every tiny detail. I swear you've timed the trip to the hospital more than once this week alone."

"Seven minutes from your place," said Hugh with a nod. "Eleven from ours."

Jake pointed to him. "On Sundays, when church is letting out, you have to add at least six minutes to each."

Hugh's eyes widened. "Noted."

Chapter Two
___

CURT RUBBED his temple as he soaked in the sight of his friends being reduced to timing hospital routes. "I'm so glad I'm not mated."

"Keep it up," said Penelope. "Kelsey and I were dusting down the basement of the antiques shop and we might have been discussing you by the crystal ball collection."

Hunted Treasures Antiques & Artifacts Shop was basically a front for a giant collection of supernatural artifacts that Wilber tended to, keeping them safe and out of the hands of madmen. He'd spent the last several months grooming his granddaughter to take over the family business. Kelsey also worked at the shop.

Curt had been in the basement of the shop a number of times. It was massive, extending under Main Street. It was packed full of the weird and the wacky. He couldn't be certain, but he was pretty sure everything in the basement was dangerous on some level.

Jake shook his head. "Warrick, if I was you, I'd demand to know what the crystal balls showed them when they were talking about you. I would *not* leave that up to chance."

Kelsey patted Jake's arm. "I still remember when it showed me you. Okay, it showed me a centaur but still. It showed me my mate. Penelope and I were talking about Curt near it, wondering when he'd meet his mate, and well, it sort of kicked on."

Curt felt the blood drain from his face. He was not ready to be tied down. "Tell me it didn't show you anyone for me."

The girls shared a look before Kelsey stepped closer to him. "Oddly, it showed us a map of the state of Mississippi."

"Why on earth would it show you Mississippi?" asked Curt.

The way Penelope looked at Kelsey let Curt know the two knew far more than they were letting on. He began to ease back from them slowly. They were up to something.

Hugh moaned. "You're acting like you're going to catch something."

"Monogamy," said Jake with a snort. "Looks like he's terrified at the idea of settling down."

Nodding, Curt stared wide-eyed at his friends. "I'm happy for you guys. I am, but that life isn't for me. I have no desire to be mated. I'm so not a family man. And I'd make a horrible father. I'm selfish. Ask anyone. They'll tell you. I'm a free spirit."

"I'm with Warrick," said Petey. "We're farts in a windstorm. We go where the wind takes us. You can't hold us down."

Curt groaned, not loving being compared to gas.

Petey waved a hand behind him, near his backside. "Speaking of farts in windstorms."

Hugh shook his head and eased his wife

closer to him. He palmed her stomach. "Seriously, Penelope, I'm not comfortable going away with how far along you are in the pregnancy."

"Grandpa had that fortune teller friend of his read both Kelsey and myself. You heard her. She agreed with what the doctor said. The babies have a bit yet. Relax. And *please* go."

Kelsey glanced at Penelope and the women sighed.

Curt lifted a hand, drawing attention to himself. "I'm guessing the womenfolk are sick of you guys hovering nonstop. You're treating them like they're made of glass now that they're expecting."

"Correct me if I'm wrong, but didn't you just run to help my expecting mate too?" asked Jake.

Curt smiled. "Yes. Because I'm a gentleman, not because I think she's too delicate to handle the world. I've heard all about her ability to shoot rainbows out of her hands and liquify demons. And let's be honest, Penelope could kick the backsides of every man here if she wanted. She comes from a line of powerful hunters. She humors us."

Penelope blushed. "Kelsey comes from hunters as well."

Curt laughed. "See? They can both beat us up. And you know as well as I do that they'll call if anything changes. I'll get a plane secured if need be and get you both back to town should any little ones decide to make a liar out of the fortune teller and doctor. Feel better?"

Kelsey laughed outright. "Curt is right. We women need a break from you guys. We'll be fine here. The entire town watches out for us all. You know how they are. Plus, Jolene has already informed us that we're having dinner together nightly while you are all away."

Penelope nodded. "And Mrs. Mays will be joining us. We'll be surrounded by people."

Hugh's eyes widened. "That woman can scare the hair off a dog with her glares."

"Speaking from experience?" asked Curt.

Hugh raised a hand but this time it wasn't to hug. His hand gesture said it all.

Curt snorted.

Penelope sighed. "Do not make me force another cookie down you."

"You behave yourselves and try to have fun," said Kelsey, stepping back just as her brother pulled an old pickup truck to a stop behind Jake's SUV.

Curt had seen the truck out in front of Old Man Nelson's place. It had been on cinderblocks for ages. He was shocked to see it in running order. It was a bigger surprise to see Nelson had parted with the thing. The town council had tried on more than one occasion to talk him into removing it from his front lawn. He'd tried to have it declared a historical landmark.

That hadn't worked out.

He did trim the weeds back from it. That was as good as it had gotten, until now.

Curt eyed the man that matched him in height and build. Though that was where the similarities ended with him and Leopold "Leo" Gibbons. Curt liked to keep his hair cut in a shorter style and his haircuts weren't cheap. Leo looked like he hacked his shoulder-length dark hair off with a pair of dull scissors or a hunting knife once every few years. He'd seen the guy's table manners. He probably did. From the heads the man turned in town as far as the ladies, it was clear chicks seemed to dig the look.

Curt couldn't make sense of it all. It always appeared as if Leo rolled out of bed in the clothing he wore for the day, and he didn't vary from faded blue jeans and old, worn shirts. Plus, the man was never without his old army jacket, which had seen better days. Frankly, Curt didn't see what appealed to the ladies.

Jake headed back to the van, opened the side door, stood just inside, and then secured his bag to the luggage rack on top of the van. He stayed in that position and looked at his brother-in-law. "Leo, tell me you didn't steal Nelson's truck."

Leo merely grinned at the question and then went to his sister. He leaned, giving her a partial hug. It looked awkward to say the least. "Hey, Leo, want a peanut butter cookie?"

Hugh eyed the man. "Say no."

Leo appeared confused as he stayed close to his sister. "I don't know about all of us taking off and leaving you alone. What if evil witches attack again while we're gone?"

"Then I'll turn them into blue goo and Jolene will run over any I miss with her tow truck *again*. Worked out good the last time." Kelsey patted her brother's cheek. "Stop worrying."

"Little sister, I'm being serious. You're pregnant now. We don't know how your magic will act. It's bad enough we have to worry about your mate's inability to control the magic he got from mating with you."

Curt flashed a cocksure smile. "So, March, is what I hear true? You know, did you sneeze and have rainbow power shoot out of your hands at Sheriff Bull's squad car?"

The incident had been the talk of the town for the past two days. Apparently, when the power struck the car it made everything electric go nuts, caused the doors to open and close on their own at random, and the horn to blare nonstop. At least that was the way Curt had heard the story told.

"Oh, it's true. Jolene isn't sure she can get the thing in working order again," said Leo, answering for Jake. "You'd think with Jake being five hundred years old he'd be able to control magic when it's given to him. But no."

Jake pointed at Leo. "Keep pushing me and I'll show you what I can do."

Leo snorted. "I'm a hunter, Jake. I'll tie you to a chair in a remote cabin in the woods and make you watch the Home Shopping Network. I hear you like that."

Wilber, in an attempt to protect his granddaughter, had kidnapped Jake, tied him to a chair in a hunting cottage, turned on the Home Shopping Network, and left him there. That had been eight months ago. It was still as funny today as it was then.

Well, not to Jake.

Jake stared wide-eyed at his wife. "You told him about what Wilber did to me?"

Kelsey shook her head and laughed. "No."

"I told him. Didn't know it was a state secret or anything," said Petey with a shrug. "It's a funny story. I tell it as often as I can. Come on, how often do you hear about a super-old centaur getting bested by a hunter? Plus, the Home Shopping Network is awesome. Hugh won't let me watch it anymore. He says I buy too much stuff from it. I don't know what impulse buying is, but he says I suffer from it. Polly said there is no cream for that. Now I just get to watch *The Wizard of Oz*. Not that I'm complaining or anything. That green witch is good-looking."

Penelope and Kelsey laughed more.

Hugh looked tired.

Jake groaned.

And Leo just looked worried about his sister. Curt couldn't exactly blame the guy. She'd been targeted by a group of evil people-eating-witches several months back. Even in a town like Everlasting, where bodies dropped all the time, that was out there.

"I'm going to be just fine. And this trip will be good for you." Kelsey wrapped her arms around Leo tight and squeezed. "You need to learn to get along with my husband. I know you and Wilber have bonded, which is great, but you need to bond to the other men as well."

"I like Petey just fine," said Leo, leaving out Hugh, Jake, and Curt.

"Hey, girls, how about you get some cookies for Leo for the road? He might get hungry," said Hugh, smirking.

Curt laughed but tried to hide it. "I thought you were warning him off those."

"I was," said Hugh, staring Leo up and down. "That was before. Now I think he should eat a dozen."

"Why? Want to have a hug buddy?" asked Curt.

Hugh growled.

Curt licked his lower lip. "Want me to invite Buster along?"

Buster, the town were-rat, could get on Hugh's nerves faster than anyone else.

Hugh gasped. "No. I'll stop. Don't eat the cookies, Leo."

Confusion coated the hunter's face. "Okay, but why?"

Penelope and Kelsey shared a look that said they were hardly innocent.

Curt eyed the woman. "You already got him, didn't you?"

Petey snorted, nodding wildly. "We put his potion in his ketchup! That boy smothers it on everything."

Leo looked up. "Potion?"

Curt walked over to his bags and retrieved them. "Apparently, the girls were worried about everyone getting along. They, with the help of Petey, decided to take matters into their own hands. They made a get-along potion. It would appear they got you and Hugh."

"And Jake," added Kelsey before covering her mouth with her hands.

Jake tilted his head back and looked up at the sky. "You had to give me a witch as a mate, didn't you, Fate?"

Kelsey smiled. "Hey, I'm new to the witch thing. And you wouldn't have me any other way."

"True," said Jake, hopping off the side of the van. He walked to her and took her hand in his. "I'm not going to ask what you did. I'm just going to tell you that I love you and I promise not to kill your brother."

"As if you could," said Leo.

Curt eyed the ladies. "I think your potion needs some work. All It's done is make Hugh look like a puppet master is controlling his arms. I don't see any sign of the rest of them wanting to hug and get along."

The next Curt knew Hugh, Jake, and Leo all went to each other and did a group hug.

Curt pointed to the women. "You two are awesome!"

"Hey. It was my dirty bathwater that made the difference," added Petey, joining the group hug.

Kelsey blinked, looking shocked. "He did what? Dirty bathwater? Petey?"

Penelope blushed. "I just found out he added that to the potion."

"I had no idea he did," said Kelsey before giving Petey a thumbs-up. "Way to cover our bases."

"See. That's what I said," replied Petey proudly. "Glad it's sort of worked. We were hoping you'd just be nicer to one another. Hugging wasn't on the menu, but we'll take it as a win, for now. Who knows, maybe it will cause more feel-goods later?"

Curt looked at the alpha males all huddled together. He whipped out his cell phone and took a picture. "I really hope it does."

The men broke apart.

Jake and Leo stood there, confusion on their faces.

Hugh just looked annoyed. "Get used to it. It's a side effect of the potion apparently."

"Probably one of many," said Petey, nothing but pride in his voice. "I should warn you all that I'm a sympathetic crier. If one of you cries, I will join in."

"We are not criers," said Jake as he teared up. He gasped. "Kelsey?"

She tugged at her lower lip. "That was mentioned as a possible by-product. Sorry. Look at it this way, you're getting in touch with your feelings."

Petey teared up too and patted Jake's shoulder before pulling an old, ratty handkerchief from his pocket and thrusting it in Jake's face. "Here."

Jake pushed it away. "Thanks. I'm good."

"Suit yourself," said Petey, blowing his nose before composing himself. "We weren't sure the potion would even work."

Hugh stared at Petey. "You cooked up a potion and you weren't sure if it would work? Do I even want to know what the possible side effects of your experiment could have been?"

Petey chuckled. "Probably not. You haven't noticed any mange, have you?"

"Petey!" shouted Hugh, going at the older man.

Curt ran interference, as was often the case when it came to Hugh's temper. "Take a breather here. You're fine. Sure, you're now a hugger who may or may not break down in tears, but that's nothing really. All is fine. Well, unless you have in fact noticed issues with mange."

"Warrick," warned Hugh.

Curt laughed. "What? It's funny. Admit it. Want to hug?"

"I don't find my wife's new interest in potion making amusing."

Penelope put a hand on her hip and stared at her husband.

Curt pointed at her since Hugh was too busy glowering to notice the dirty look Penelope had set upon him. When he did, his shoulders slumped. "I love your hobby. Did I say otherwise? Silly me. I really hope you mix more potions. Can't wait to try them."

Petey leaned and put the back of his hand to the side of his mouth and did the loudest whisper known to man. "I'm not sure she buys it. It lacked a level of believability. Want me to back you up? We men gotta stick together. Two peas in a pod."

Curt sighed. If Petey was starting with the idioms already, the trip was going to be a long one. The man was a walking book of them.

"Thanks, but I think she heard you," returned Hugh, nodding in the direction of his mate.

Petey whistled, put his hands behind his

Don't Stop Bewitching

back as he rocked on the balls of his feet. "Some weather we're having, huh?"

Just then Wilber Messing came out of the front door of his antiques shop. He had a wooden crate in his arms.

Hugh hurried to him and tried to take it.

"Boy, do I look like I can't handle this?" snapped the white-haired, rosy-cheeked man who was two hundred years old but didn't look to be out of his early sixties.

Hugh grumbled. "Fine. Have it your way, you old grump."

Just then Hugh's arms went out and he twisted fast, hugging Petey in place of Wilber.

Curt couldn't breathe for a moment as a bout of laughter overtook him.

"Grandpa," said Penelope. "Be nice."

Wilber rolled his eyes and thrust the crate at Hugh. "If you can find time in between holding Petey, you can carry this. Try not to drop it. You could start the apocalypse if any of the artifacts in it break. If that Destiny Vase so much as cracks, we're all screwed."

Hugh ended up having to pry Petey off him so he could take the crate.

"End of the world," said Curt with another laugh.

Wilber didn't join in.

Curt's eyes widened. "For real?"

Wilber gave him a look that said, "wouldn't you like to know."

"This is going to be great. Just great," said Curt as he followed Jake's previous steps to secure his luggage to the rack on top of the van. He put his hands out to Hugh, waiting as the wolf-shifter handed him the crate.

"Are you crazy?" shouted Wilber, causing Hugh to fumble, drop the crate, and then dive down in an attempt to break its fall.

Curt did the same, throwing himself to the ground and sliding his hands under the crate to try to stop a possible apocalypse.

The two alpha males ended up side by side, on the ground, basically holding hands under the crate, their faces pressed to the bottom portion of the van.

"Oh, look at that. They're getting along

great. Potion worked like a charm," said Petey with a grin as he walked towards his pickup truck.

Curt got to his feet and helped Hugh to stand, each babying the crate and sharing a look between them.

Wilber strutted past, took the crate, and put it inside the van. "Want something done, you have to do it yourself. Shifters. Good for nothing."

Penelope cleared her throat.

Wilber sighed. "Fine. They're good for something. I can't think of anything off the top of my head right now, but I'm sure there is something. Oh I know. Their pelts make warm coats."

"They do," said Leo with a nod.

"Oh yeah. This trip is going to go over great," said Curt with a shake of his head.

Chapter Three

THREE DAYS LATER...

Missi (Mississippi) Peugeot put the last of the new shipment of candles in the display holders at her magic shop—Charmed Life Magik Shop. She'd come in early to get a head start on inventory for the month and to restock anything she was low on. Since she'd been busy helping with preparations for the upcoming town Founder's Day Celebration, her time had been split between the shop and planning duties. While she wasn't the best at remembering things like her shoes, or where she left her bicycle, she was good about keeping her store stocked with goods.

Two high school students worked for her during the summer months and would be in for work in about an hour and half, when the shop actually opened for business. She'd yet to train them to do inventory. It was on her ever-growing to-do list. First up, it was get the shop's inventory restocked and order anything she might need and then it was time to finish making the decorations for the town square.

This year's Founder's Day motif was shifter themed, so they were making cardboard cutouts of various animals, covering them in glitter, and then stringing them from lampposts around town. It hadn't been her idea, but she'd somehow gotten stuck doing the work. Last year they'd featured the vampires and the year before that it was the spirits so the shifters were feeling a bit left out.

She didn't think glitter cutouts would make them feel included and valued, but she'd been outvoted.

The Founder's Day celebrations were getting ready to kick off, meaning there would be a month of fun, food, games, spells, and general supernatural mishaps and hijinks. That wasn't the slogan, but it should have been.

Missi reassessed the candle section, which took up an entire shelving unit, noting that the ritual candles were still low even with the new stock put out. It was painfully clear she'd not ordered enough. She pulled her small, ever-present notepad from the pocket of her long skirt and jotted down a note to call her cousin for more.

Her cousin was a local candlemaker. Beatrice sold candles globally, thanks to the World Wide Web, and was in high demand. As a natural-born witch from a powerful line, Beatrice was able to create candles infused with actual magic, increasing their effectiveness tremendously. That also increased demand for her product. It was next to impossible to keep the shelves stocked. The time was fast approaching for Beatrice to expand her operations to something larger than the back of her house.

Telling that to Beatrice was easier said than done.

Missi had always seen herself as stuck in

her ways. A creature of habit. Beatrice made her look downright free-spirited and up for anything.

"Call Bee and get more chime candles," Missi said, unconcerned with the fact she was talking to herself. "Check in with Mr. Flanks about his fall line of cauldrons."

She sighed, adding that to her notepad as well before shoving it back into her oversized pocket. Her list was always growing.

Missi lifted the crate that the candles had come in and took it behind the counter to give to her cousin later. Both women were big into reducing waste and avoiding things such as single-use plastics. Neither drove a car to cut down on emissions, and Beatrice went as far as to have solar panels on her small home, serving as her only power source. The effort would have been great if not for the fact that Beatrice lived on the edge of the forest and had a semi-shady lot. Ironically enough, she often had to use her own candles to see by when it got dark and she was out of stored solar energy.

No thank you. Missi would stick with the modern convenience of electricity.

Missi went to the counter and gathered the newest white sage bundles and took them to the three-tiered basket that sat off to the side of the front register. The bottom basket was the largest and held the biggest of the bundles. The next level up held the medium-sized ones, and the top basket held the small bundles. She never quite understood what the point of the smallest ones were, but they sold well. She finished refilling the baskets and then stepped back, surveying her handiwork. It looked perfect.

The shop had once been run by her mother, as it had been in her family for generations. The torch had passed to Missi almost two years ago and while she'd been reluctant to take the reins, fearing the townspeople would balk at change, she had to admit that her mother and grandmother had been right when they'd insisted she take over.

It had become an unofficial town landmark because it was sort of hard to miss.

It was large and round.

A perfect circle that sat nestled in the middle of the French and Spanish-inspired architecture that was common to the region. Like the French Quarter in New Orleans, which was just a short jaunt down the road, Hedgewitch Cove had a certain old-world charm, from its European influences to its emphasis on community.

The shop had become a part of her. An extension of herself. She couldn't see herself doing anything else. Though, like the rest of her siblings and cousins, she still pitched in where she was needed at the various businesses her family owned around Hedgewitch Cove.

Both sides of her family could be traced back to the start of the town; each were part of the founding families. On her father's side, the Peugeots had long and proud Southern roots, deeply ingrained in Louisiana. Her mother's side, the Caillats, could be traced back to France and had roots in witchcraft.

The Caillats, along with three other powerful lines of witches who called the town home, had combined their efforts at the town's creation and made sure it was a safe haven for supernaturals. The spell they'd worked kept almost all humans out. It compelled anyone without supernatural blood in them to keep on moving. To not notice the town, or the signs for it. To not see it on a map.

Yes, humans tended to wander in every now and again, but by and large, Hedgewitch Cove was mainly filled with supernaturals. The few humans who got lost and somehow managed to circumvent the wards didn't stay long and once they left, memories of the town and its inhabitants left them.

There were many towns like Hedgewitch Cove all over the world. They were safe havens for those who were different.

Like she was.

And she loved it.

Missi loved everything about Hedgewitch Cove and every eccentric member of it. There was no other place she could see herself calling home. Unlike some of her siblings and cousins, Missi didn't long to explore the world or put down roots somewhere new.

No.

She loved the security blanket the town provided. Loved being able to set her watch by the actions and workings of the town. Even if they weren't actually all related to her (though it often seemed they were), they were family to her and she cared deeply for them all. Even down to the crotchety old men who sat outside of the barbershop in the morning, reading their newspapers, sipping coffee, and commenting loudly on the youth today and how much humans were mucking up everything.

They pretty much thought the world was going to hell in a handbasket.

Since Hedgewitch Cove had an actual portal to hell within it, that wasn't a stretch by any means. They had a portal to a number of magical realms as well, so no one really batted an eye about it all. Though they did have the occasional issue with random demons strolling through town square. Unicorns and pixies were a common occurrence too as it seemed the portal to their realm tended to open the most. Pixies got into more trouble than any other magical group she could think of.

Such was the way of it in Hedgewitch Cove. It simply was what it was. She'd never actually lived anywhere else and always found it odd when she visited a town full of humans that they never seemed to see the magic and beauty that surrounded them. If they but stopped and glanced around, they'd see everyday wonders.

"I'm so happy I'm not human," she said as she grabbed a dusting cloth and cleaned the back shelf of dragon figurines.

Humans had, at one point, tried a number of her ancestors for witchcraft. When she was little, her older brothers would tell her stories of humans and how they'd search out little witch girls, stuff them full of treats and sweets only to eat them. It wasn't until Missi was in her teens that she found the fairy tale was actually a human one and in it, the witch was doing the fattening up of the children to eat them later, not the other way around. But two of her brothers, New York (York) and Louisiana (Louis), had found it much funnier to twist the tale and scare her. As the baby of the family, she tended to be the butt end of numerous jokes her siblings played.

The bell to the front door chimed as it opened, drawing her attention. She never locked her door. It felt unwelcoming and wrong.

"Blasted dog! If Luc doesn't get you fixed, I'm gonna do it myself. That'll teach you. Always diggin'. You get on now. Mississippi doesn't want you tearin' up her rosemary plants!" Cherry Corduas hurried in, shutting the door behind her, looking slightly disheveled before opening the door again, looking out and pointing. "Don't go givin' me that look, Furfur. You'll be fur-less if you keep it up. I'll be having words with your daddy. Devil or not, he's gotta make his dog mind."

She slammed the door as best she could with a huff and then straightened herself. The woman, who was in her early fifties, wore a floor-length navy-blue skirt with small pink flowers on it and a bright pink flowing shirt. She had more necklaces around her neck than Missi could count, each representing about every religion one could think of, and had her blonde hair piled high on her head. Thick yellow plastic-framed glasses with small pink and blue polka-dots sat perched on the end of her nose.

The woman had been offbeat ever since Missi could recall. Ms. Cherry had once dressed as an ornamental hedge for a town function. Missi had loved it. Though it had been a bit of an issue when a bird flew into the outfit and tried to make itself right at home.

Ms. Cherry taught middle school English during the day, and in the evenings she taught drama classes at the small local theater. It was no secret the woman had dreams of one day being on stage, in front of the masses. For now, Ms. Cherry had to settle for Hedgewitch Cove, population too small to bother counting.

She gave a wide smile and rechecked her hair with her hands before blowing out a long breath. "Mississippi, how's your mornin'?"

"Good, thank you for asking. I take it Furfur is getting into trouble again," said

Missi, already knowing the animal, who was actually a hellhound but looked like a boxer dog, tended to find mischief anywhere he could. He was basically harmless. Though he did have a digging fetish and was known to run off with important items only to bury them later. The town employed a man whose sole job was to go around Hedgewitch Cove searching for all the stolen items, uncover them, and return them to their rightful owners.

Ms. Cherry scowled. "Luc had best do somethin' with that mongrel. Obedience trainin' or a leash. Somethin'. The boy needs to learn to control his dog."

Missi hid her laugh. Luc, the "boy" Ms. Cherry was ranting about, was actually Lucifer (Luc) Dark, otherwise known in most circles as the devil himself. "You know the saying, while the devil's away, Furfur will play."

"Then the demons he has runnin' his inn ought to take better care of the thing. I think it has fleas," snapped Ms. Cherry.

Missi covered her smile with her hand. "I'm sure Furfur does not have fleas."

She smoothed the front of her skirt and took a deep breath. "I'm a cat person myself."

"Yes, I know. How are Toil and Trouble? Did they love the new toys you got for them?"

Ms. Cherry's cats were somewhat notorious around town. She often walked them in a baby stroller and had been known to put tiny conical hats on their head to "protect them from the sun." They were spoiled through and through. A sister and brother pair, the boy, Trouble, was all black with a white bowtie-looking mark on his upper chest. His sister, Toil, was reversed, all white with a black bowtie mark. Ms. Cherry would never admit to as much, but the cats were known to instigate poor Furfur.

Missi had once caught them ganging up on the dog just outside of town square, in the wooded area that ran all the way back to Dead Man's Creek. Furfur was surprisingly gentle with cats, more than likely because Luc had commanded it, so the dog made no effort to defend itself. Missi had brought Furfur back to the shop, tended to his scratched-open nose and ear, and then walked him back to Hells Gate Inn, the place he called home.

Ms. Cherry's smile widened. "Oh, they love the new toys. Thanks so much for getting' them in. Not many magic shops bother thinkin' about stockin' items for familiars. You're so thoughtful. You're your momma up one side and down the other."

"Thank you. I'm an animal lover. Actually, I love everything to do with nature," said Missi before pointing in the direction of the other side of the shop. "There are some new cat toys back there if you want to have a look."

Ms. Cherry's eyes lit up as she hurried in the direction of the pet section.

Chapter Four

MISSI PULLED out her ledger and began to mark down what items she'd restocked thus far, what she still needed to put out, and what she needed to order more of. She wasn't a fan of computers in her store and preferred to keep a written record. Her brother Louis wholeheartedly supported her decision as he was convinced technology was the devil. It was a wonder he permitted electricity to be in his home and the antiques shop he ran. Had the phone not already been installed, Missi wasn't sure Louis would have allowed even that.

She didn't go quite that far.

She had a business phone and a cell

phone. Of course, she rarely remembered to charge her cell, which made it hard for her to be reached. And then there was the fact she often forgot her cell around town. People were used to her, and the phone always managed to find its way back to her one way or another.

Missi skimmed her finger over the ledger listings, making sure she hadn't missed anything. Dragon's blood was low, and she didn't have any in stock. She made note of that and then continued to go over the ledger. When she was satisfied, she closed the book and put it under the counter near the front register.

"Need any help with anything?" she called out.

There was no reply.

"Ms. Cherry?"

Still nothing.

Perplexed, she headed towards the pet section at the far back of the shop. It was empty. Since the shop was a large circle with floor-to-ceiling shelves and small nook areas, it was easier to get lost in it than one would think. That being said, surely she'd have seen Ms. Cherry from the front counter near the door if the woman had left.

She hadn't.

"Ms. Cherry?"

Still nothing.

Missi continued and pushed back the long strands of red beads that hung in place of a door, leading to the back-office area and the restroom. There was also a small room off the office where Missi kept some of the objects that were just for darker magic. As a shop that catered to magics, she stocked anything they'd need. That included some questionable items. She didn't leave those out for just anyone to happen on. No. She made sure they were tucked away.

Ms. Cherry wouldn't have dared go into that room. Not with her line of witches having a sordid past with the dark arts.

Missi continued to hold the beads aside as she stood in the doorway. Her brother York, who was Louis's twin, often called them her hippie beads. He also called her a flower child so there was that. In his mind the fact she gravitated towards long shirts and dresses, wanted to protect the environment, didn't eat red meat, and felt at one with nature made her a hippie. He liked jeans, T-shirts, steak, beer, and hunting.

They had very little in common.

She entered the back office and glanced around. There was no sign of Ms. Cherry. The restroom door was standing wide open and the light was off. The back door to the shop was closed, bolted from the inside.

A hand fell upon her shoulder and Missi nearly leapt out of her skin. She spun around and touched her upper chest as she looked at Ms. Cherry, positive her heart was going to pop clean out of her. "Jumping jellybeans!"

Ms. Cherry's eyes widened. "Mississippi, heavens to Betsey. You're jumpier than a frog on a lily pad in a pond full of gators."

"You startled me," she managed, feeling foolish. "Do you need any help with anything?"

"Oh goddess, no. I know my way around this shop like the back of my hand. I've been comin' here since I was knee-high, and your grandmother ran it. Then I was a loyal customer all through the decades your momma was in charge," Ms. Cherry said, moving over to the candles that Missi had only just restocked. She lifted a seven-day black ritual candle, bringing it to her nose and smelling it.

Some thought black candles always meant black magic, but that wasn't necessarily the case. In fact, black candles were often used to rid negative energy from an area, for protection, to clear a space, to cleanse auras, and more, not just stress and chaos.

"These are new," said Ms. Cherry. "They smell amazin' and the magic infused in them has a touch of whimsy."

She was right. They were a newer version of the black candles Beatrice normally made. "Bee swears they're better."

"Oh, I bet they are. She is so gifted," replied Ms. Cherry. She then began to look over the new white seven-day candles as well. "I'll take one of each. I'll need a green, red, and purple as well. Can't very well be gettin' one without the other."

Missi went to an endcap and retrieved a basket. She carried it to Ms. Cherry and handed it to her.

Ms. Cherry took it and placed the candles she wanted within it.

"Looking to dress the candles with anything in particular?" asked Missi.

Dressing a candle by way of rubbing it with specific oils helped to increase the candle's power and intention. Missi prided herself on her homemade oils. She spent hours poring over recipes and trying various combinations. Spells and potions came naturally to her.

Ms. Cherry paused, seeming reluctant to comment further. "Have you made any new attraction oils lately? The ones you did around the Yule were wonderful."

"I have." Missi went to the shelves full of oils and found what Ms. Cherry was looking for. "I think you're going to really like the updated formula I'm using. But I'd suggest going with a smaller amount than normal for any spell work. The new makeup of it all really goes a long way with just a little."

"My philosophy is the more the merrier," responded Ms. Cherry. "Tell me, Mississippi, you didn't happen to hear that ruckus the other night, did you?"

Ms. Cherry lived a few doors down from the magic shop. Since Missi lived above the shop that meant they were neighbors. Two houses were between them. One belonged to the man who owned the iron factory and the other belonged to a former pirate. Both of whom tended to be very quiet neighbors. "No. I didn't hear anything for the last few nights. The new tea I put together is for sleep and I've been testing it all week. Worked too well if I say so myself. I'm going to need to tweak it a touch. Had Winston not woken me, I'm sure I'd still be asleep."

At the mention of Missi's familiar, who happened to be a parrot, Ms. Cherry beamed. "How is Winston doin'? He hasn't made any great escapes lately, so I've not seen him. Toil and Trouble always keep a close watch out the window. You know how much they like to chase poor Winston."

Missi cringed inwardly. Actually, it was

Winston who chased the cats. There was nothing more embarrassing than knowing your familiar was a bully. "He's doing well. He is no longer whistling classic rock songs. Remind me to thank York for that again."

Ms. Cherry laughed. "York cares for you, as a brother should. He's different from Louis and Arizona. Louis has no issue sharin' his feelings. Arizona, when he's home, is loud in every aspect of his life. That includes makin' his thoughts and feelings known. York is more like your father than the other two. He keeps his emotions tucked away like a squirrel with a nut. Thinks it's not manly to make 'em known. That's hogwash."

Missi agreed but had long since given up trying to change her brother.

Ms. Cherry eyed her. "When I ran into your mother last week, she said Arizona wasn't plannin' to come home for Founder's Day. That so?"

Arizona, her oldest sibling, had decided small town Southern life wasn't for him. He'd gone off to see the world and sent postcards home every week. That had been the only real communication they'd had with him in months. Missi knew it bothered their mother, so much so their father was close to tracking the boy down and dragging him home by his ear.

"I haven't talked to him about Founder's Day. I think York has. I'll ask when I see York later today," said Missi, wanting to get off the subject.

"What about Georgia? You talk with her lately?"

Georgia was Missi's oldest sister. She no longer resided in Hedgewitch Cove either. "No. She and Louis talk a lot though. So, what ruckus happened the other night?"

Ms. Cherry leaned in as if someone might overhear. "There was a lot of hollerin' and carrin' on before there was a big boom. It shook my house. Now, I'm not one to gossip, but I could have sworn Blackbeard and Mr. Flanks were the ones doing the yellin'. But I didn't see so I can't really say for certain. I'm sure there's a story there. I'm shocked you didn't hear it or feel it. I'm goin' to need a bag of that tea."

Missi hadn't heard a thing. The men she

mentioned had a history of disagreements. They argued over everything from Blackbeard's choice of businesses to the shared fence on their lot line. It had never come to blows or booms before, that she was aware. "Blackbeard normally stops by the shop on his day's off. He didn't do that this week."

"I haven't seen him around since all the commotion. But you know how moody he can get. Pirates," said Ms. Cherry with a sigh.

She was right. Blackbeard did tend to get moody. Most thought he was gruff. Missi knew better.

Ms. Cherry glanced at the oils. "Have any more of that suppression one you made last summer?"

Nodding, Missi opened the bottom cabinet portion of the shelving unit and looked around for the oil in question. She found a small glass jar and stood. She hesitated before handing over the oils.

Ms. Cherry came from a line of witches who didn't have the best in the way of reputations. She and her sisters all still resided in town despite whispers that they were as their ancestors had been, up to no good. And while the notion was absurd that she was anything like the witches of old, it was hard to ignore the feeling Missi was getting. Could it be that Ms. Cherry was working with dark magic?

It wasn't against the law per se, and dabbling in the dark arts didn't mean one was necessarily evil. Missi had once been asked to help with a spell that fell over the line but it had been for a good reason. It was for a town newcomer who'd needed help controlling his newly developed shifter side. Since his shifter form had taken lives, the spell needed to help him gain initial control over it, in order to then learn to do so naturally. It had required a bit more power than normal. Dark magic was brought in, but it had been for a greater good.

That wasn't always the case. It just depended on how the dark magic was used. If it was to kill someone, then yes, that was illegal. But there were a lot of gray areas within the realm of magic and supernaturals. This was shaping up to be one of those. "I know better than anyone that it's impolite to ask about what spell another witch is working on, but is there anything I can help with?"

"Oh no, sugar. I've got it covered. But thank you for the offer."

With that, Missi nodded and headed back to the counter. She busied herself with some light cleaning while Ms. Cherry continued to fill her hand basket.

The door to the shop opened again and Jasmine Harris peeked in. Her long, curly hair was down today and looked amazing. Her dark gaze found Missi and she smiled. "I know you're not open just yet. I'm here on town council business."

Missi eyed her longtime friend. She'd gone to school with Jasmine and had known the woman since they were babies. Jasmine's mother was a voodoo priestess and her father was a were-panther, who was also the high school football coach. Her mother ran a daycare that was next to the school and always had a full house. Everyone loved her mom. The town loved her father so long as the football team was winning. Since it was the South, they took football very seriously.

"Oh no. Please don't tell me that Barnebas is trying to get another vote to force me to sell the lot behind me so he can expand the post office."

Jasmine clicked her tongue on her inner cheek and hurried towards the counter with a clipboard in hand. "It's worse."

Worse than the local mailman campaigning to take her property for the post office? The man had been trying for two straight years. He'd even commissioned billboards. She'd tried hard to talk him into looking at property out near the wooded section of town, but he wouldn't hear of any such thing. It probably didn't help that the woods were known as a dangerous area and had a long, ugly past.

Jasmine handed Missi the clipboard. "I read your cards this morning and you're about to have some major changes in your life. My spirit guides are telling me that there is some loophole with that back lot and someone, not Barnebas, has an interest in it. I did some digging and it turns out there is some rich big shot from out of town who has his eye on it. Wants to develop it commercially. Sign here. I'm starting a petition to stop it."

"You're getting signatures to stop something from happening that hasn't even started yet?" asked Missi, signing her full name on the form. Surprisingly, Jasmine already had a full sheet of names and the day had only just started.

"You bet your bottom dollar I am. When I learned about it all, it made me angrier than a puffed toad," said Jasmine proudly.

"I love that you worry about me," said Missi. "But I'm sure everything will be fine."

Jasmine didn't look convinced. "I've been sensing something off with your aura. This must be it."

Missi shook her head and laughed.

"Yuck it up now, but when some random guy comes out of nowhere and gets his hands on your back lot, you'll be sorry. That sounded dirty. But you know what I mean."

Missi rolled her eyes playfully. "I'll stand my ground. No big shot is running over me."

"Good girl," said Jasmine. "Okay, I'm off to get more signatures. I plan to make Barnebas sign. Trust me, if he can't have the lot, he won't want anyone else to either."

That sounded about right.

"Goddess willing and the creek don't rise, I'll get this stopped before it gets started," said Jasmine as she waved and rushed out of the shop.

"Was that Jasmine I just heard?" asked Ms. Cherry from the back of the store.

"Yes, ma'am. She's gathering signatures to stop my back lot from falling into some unknown rich person's hands because of a loophole."

Ms. Cherry appeared with a full basket in hand. "Well, we can't let that happen. You have the best garden back there. Tell me who I need to curse. Want him to have the pox or stop breathin' for good?"

Missi stiffened.

A strange expression moved over the

woman's face. "Sugar, I was only kiddin'. I don't curse people…*anymore*."

"Oh, I almost forgot," said Missi quickly, wanting to get off the subject of curses. "I put out new sage bundles. I have small ones. I know you like them."

Cherry went right for the display containing the bundled sage. "Your mother's sage is simply the best for cleansings. I don't know how Murielle does it, but I've never found better. Every herb she grows is simply perfect. Honestly, every one of you Caillat witches are so talented with the craft."

"Thank you. Momma will be pleased to hear you like her sage. You know how she's been worried about the newest shop in the French Quarter opening."

"No self-respectin' member of the community would be caught dead there. That is a tourist trap. It won't be long before the legit magic shops and practitioners there drive that bogus one out." Ms. Cherry placed three small bundles of sage on the counter and then set her full basket there as well. She glanced at a small tray full of travel-size banishing oils. She took four and set them with her other items.

Missi lifted a brow, having seen the woman purchase the exact items not long back. "Ms. Cherry, you wouldn't be planning on banishing Rockey *again*, would you?"

She blushed, touched her necklaces, and made a big production of staring around the shop. "Oh, are those new essential oils?"

"Ms. Cherry," stressed Missi.

Ms. Cherry sighed. "Fine. Yes. That old goat is makin' fun of my actin' again."

"Your acting is amazing," said Missi, though in truth it wasn't the best. It came from the heart and that was really all that mattered.

"Who is he to judge me? So what if he had a run on an off-off-Broadway show nearly seventy years ago?" She huffed. "I shouldn't have to be subjected to him because he had a sandbag fall on his head while on stage how many years ago? There are days I wonder if someone wasn't aimin' for him. If he lectures me one more time on the finer points of Shakespeare, I swear I won't be held accountable for my actions. He's a Midsummer's Night Nightmare."

Rockey Bigelow considered himself something of a celebrity and didn't let the town forget. Every chance he could, he proudly declared himself to be a Shakespearean trained actor with stage experience. It would have been easier to swallow if he didn't sound like he was starring in *The Sopranos*. Somehow, a mobster accent didn't really lend itself to serious stage productions.

That didn't stop Rockey.

Neither did death. He was no longer a member of the living. It was hard to get the world to see your acting genius when they couldn't actually see you. He'd been the star of a play that had passed through the local theater seventy years ago, and an unfortunate backdrop incident left him an eternal resident of the town.

Hedgewitch Cove considered itself one of the most haunted towns in the world. Missi had never really looked more into it, but she had to think the claim wasn't that far off base. Rockey, unlike some of the spirits who called the town home, wasn't bound to one location. He could roam about freely within the town limits. And from the expression on Ms. Cherry's face, he'd been hanging at the theater again.

Missi almost felt bad for the woman. Still, banishing wasn't the answer. Rockey was annoying, but that was taking it to the extreme.

"Ms. Cherry, the last time you banished him from the theater we had to sit through a four-hour-long town council meeting, hearing arguments from both sides, vote, tally said votes, and then three different covens, along with Blackbeard, had to help lift the spell," Missi said, offering a warm smile in an attempt to get Ms. Cherry to see reason. The entire banishing fiasco of the year before was still talked about by the coffee crew, who made gossiping outside the barbershop a sport. "Maybe you and Rockey should consider some counseling rather than this."

She jutted out her chin and tapped the counter. "He started it this time."

"What happened?"

"He had the nerve to make a pipe burst in the ceiling above me as I was teachin' a class about the finer points of Shakespeare," said Ms. Cherry, reaching up and touching her hair. "There is nothin' like helpin' someone find their motivation one second and being drenched the next. You'd think he was Fate's gift to thespians with the way he carries on. And you ever heard of Shakespeare performed by a man from New Jersey? He sounds like a mobster when he talks, not Puck. I swear, that man lives to annoy me. I warned him that I'd snatch him bald if he didn't stop. He laughed."

Missi bit her lower lip. Her mother had told her once that the man had ties to the Mafia back in the day and it was rumored that the backdrop misfortune wasn't an accident at all. Missi didn't pry further. "Um, he doesn't live at all. I think he might miss being a contributing member of society. Maybe having him assist in teaching a few classes would help that. Have you ever considered it?"

She looked appalled at the proposition.

Missi sighed and rang up the items

before bagging them. It was too much to hope for peace between Rockey and Ms. Cherry. They'd been at each other's throats for far too long.

Ms. Cherry handed her cash and then paused, pushing her yellow glasses up her nose. "Somethin' has changed about you. What is it?"

Missi watched the woman. "Nothing that I'm aware of."

Ms. Cherry glanced around the shop and the edges of her mouth drew upwards. In the next instant, the woman was behind the counter and hugging Missi tight, smashing her necklaces against Missi in the process. "Oh bless you, sugar! I'm so happy for you both!"

"Um, thank you?" Missi wasn't sure what she was being hugged for.

Ms. Cherry released her only to hug her again, this time tearing up. "Oh, young love does a heart good."

"Young love?" asked Missi with a slight yelp. She was not in love. She wasn't even in like. In fact, she was about as far from love as one could get. She did not have a boyfriend or a special man friend.

Missi had once fallen for the charms of an out-of-towner who had been visiting Hedgewitch Cove on holiday. He'd raced into town in an expensive foreign car, had been dressed in fancy, expensive clothes, and had a smile that could charm the coldest of hearts.

He also had an eye for other women and no desire to call Hedgewitch Cove home for life. Each time they'd argue about it, the guy would show up with flowers and jewelry. He'd thought money solved everything.

It didn't fix shallow and materialistic.

Missi had learned her lesson with the guy and had sworn off rich men from that point forward. They were nothing but trouble.

Ms. Cherry released her and stepped back, still grinning. "I'm so excited. I gotta go find your grandmother right away. She has to be beside herself over the good news."

"Not to sound ungrateful for your kind

words, but what are you talking about? I'm not in love," said Missi. "I'm not even dating. Not since You-Know-Who."

Ms. Cherry's lips pursed. "We won't discuss him. Thinks because he drives fancy cars and buys you expensive jewelry that he can buy your affection and make you leave us."

So much for not discussing You-Know-Who.

Ms. Cherry tipped her head as if listening to something only she could hear. It was a well-known fact that the Corduas had deep ties to magic in the community as well, though their coven had been disbanded nearly two centuries back. No one really said why, but Missi got the impression it was because they'd practiced dark magic. Ms. Cherry winked. "You will be. *Very* soon. He's on his way now. Careful or you're likely to be hit by flower power."

"Flower what? And who is on his way?" asked Missi, her heart rate speeding.

"Why, your mate, of course," said Ms. Cherry before hugging her quickly again. The woman took her bag and rushed in the direction of the door, mumbling something about hunting down Missi's grandmother and then banishing "the Capone wannabe" from the theater for a week to teach him a lesson.

Missi stood there, watching the woman rush off down the street, in the direction of the cemetery. Ms. Cherry knew Missi's grandmother well. This time of the day she'd be at the cemetery putting fresh flowers on graves before enjoying a spot of tea with her fellow Historical Society Members—a number of which were deceased.

The phone rang and Missi jumped in place before letting out a shaky breath and going for the phone. She laughed slightly as she answered it. "Charmed Life Magik Shop, how can I help you?"

"Missi, my flight just got in and I'm running behind. I only just landed in New Orleans. I swear I had two layovers, missed a connecting flight and then my plane needed maintenance. I think this trip is cursed. My car isn't where I parked it in the long-term parking lot. The security guard thinks I forgot where I parked. Anyway, the delivery man is at the restaurant already. He needs to be let in. Can you run over?" asked her sister Virginia. "Louis was supposed to but he's not answering his phone. I tried Momma, but I can't get in touch with her. Daddy is on a call. Mémé will be out of pocket while she has tea and seances."

"With Founder's Day events kicking off, the restaurant can't miss a delivery and this guy is human. The spell Momma helped me cast over him only keeps him from noticing the weird around here for a limited time. I don't even want to think what would happen if Headless Hank decides to go for a morning run, just as the spell on the delivery guy wears off. Can you imagine? I'm going to wring Louis's neck when I see him. He swore to me he'd handle it if my flight was delayed. I'm always covering his deliveries for the antiques shop. The least he could do was return the favor. He's probably avoiding my calls."

"Louis never carries his cell phone," said Missi, surprised she was able to get a word in edgewise considering how much

Virginia liked to talk. Virginia was a Type A personality and it showed. Just once Missi wished her sister would lighten up, let her hair down, and simply be.

That would take a miracle, or one heck of a spell.

"Grr, you're right," said Virginia. "Our brother is the worst with cell phones."

He was the type of person who got lost in history books and loved antiques. He liked simpler times, when people connected face-to-face rather than on the internet—something he refused to have at his home. It had taken the entire family to talk him into even owning a cell phone. They'd forgotten to bargain with him to actually turn the thing on and carry it with him.

"My girls aren't in just yet to open the shop," said Missi as she checked the time. "Can York do it?"

"He's not answering his cell either and last I heard he was heading out for a big catch. Something about getting approved for a bigger haul," said Virginia, apprehension in her voice.

"Did you really try York or are you

afraid Sigmund will answer and you might have to actually speak to the man?" asked Missi.

Hedgewitch Cove was a safe haven for the supernatural. Sigmund Bails was a man who had come by way of a trusted friend, in need of assistance and guidance. The kind only other supernaturals could provide. Missi didn't know exactly what had happened in the man's past, but she did know Sigmund had not gone unnoticed by her sister.

"No," squeaked Virginia quickly before clearing her throat. "I mean, yes, I tried him and no, I'm not worried about Sig answering."

"Okay, if that is what you want to go with," said Missi with a grin.

"I could ask Thom to help me this morning if it's too much of a bother for you."

Missi cringed at the idea. The last time Thom—who owned the bookstore that was close to Runes, the restaurant her family owned, and Virginia ran and operated—had helped, he'd nearly burned the restaurant down by accident. He'd bumped a burner, turned it on, filled the kitchen with gas and then left. "It's better if I just run over. Charmed doesn't officially open for another hour. I should be able to get there and back before then."

"You are the best, sis," said Virginia before she made a strange noise. "Missi, is there something different going on with you?"

Missi tensed, thinking about Ms. Cherry's strange behavior. "W-what do you mean?"

"I don't know. I just got a weird vibe and then the strangest urge to congratulate you," replied Virginia. "I didn't sleep well and had a layover so take that as you may."

They came from a long line of powerful Caillat witches. Their vibes generally weren't to be toyed with or ignored. Coupled with Ms. Cherry's rather odd visit, Missi peered around the shop, half-worried her future husband would suddenly be standing there—whoever he might be. "Do not tell me I'm about to meet Mr. Right.

I've already heard all about it and it's not happening. Flower Power my hiney."

"Wait. What?" asked Virginia. "I leave town for one week and you find Mr. Right and flower power while I'm gone?"

Missi laughed. "I'm not finding anyone. I was just informed by Ms. Cherry, who is in the process of trying to banish Rockey *again*, that Mr. Right is on his way here as we speak."

Virginia grew quiet on the other end of the phone. "Tell me you put some makeup on this morning and you're not trying that natural look thing you're so fond of. You are wearing shoes, right? You're not doing that back-to-nature barefoot thing again, are you?"

Missi shook her head. "Stop it."

"What? I find out my sister is about to meet Mr. Right, I'm allowed to want you to look your best and have on shoes."

"I'm hanging up now and heading over to Runes. You owe me big," said Missi as she disengaged the call.

Chapter Five

"PETEY, what did you eat this morning?" demanded Hugh as he tried but failed to get one of the windows in the back of the Volkswagen van to pop open. From the rate in which the wolf-shifter was hitting at it, he'd save time and rip the door off the hinges sooner, rather than later.

Curt coughed and pounded on his chest. The smell burned his nose. He wasn't sure, but there was a high likelihood that his sense of smell might end up damaged beyond repair.

Petey really did have issues. His fart in the windstorm-ness was going to the extreme.

Curt waved his hand back and forth. "That is not natural. Should we take him to see a doctor or something? That has to be a sign of something terminal, right?"

Petey, who had called shotgun, turned and looked at them from the passenger seat. "Breaking wind is natural. If you hold it in, you'll blow up. I knew a guy who did that once and only once. Instead of letting his wind break, he kept it all in. He popped like he was a balloon, and someone had stuck him with a pin. One second he was there, the next he was deflating and floating away. Made the loudest sound I've ever heard in my life. Shame really. He'd been a nice guy. I wonder where he ended up? Think he landed in Canada? He was headed north. Anyone know the Mounties' policy on deflated men?"

"Petey, no one you knew blew up from holding their gas in," said Hugh as he plugged his nose.

"Did so," protested Petey. "You don't know about him because he's from the place we're headed. And what happens in

Don't Stop Bewitching

Hedgewitch Cove stays in Hedgewitch Cove."

"Sure he is," said Hugh with a shake of his hand. "How do you open these windows? It's hotter than Hades back here and now it smells bad too."

Curt took over and on his first try he managed to get the window to pop open. He grinned.

"I loosened it for you," said Hugh.

"Sure *you* did," returned Curt as he took in a deep breath of fresh air. He leaned back as best he could with the limited leg space the van provided. The spot wasn't comfortable, so he shifted a bit, unintentionally kicking the crate Wilber had said could end the world.

Curt froze.

Hugh gasped.

Jake sat up fast from his spot in the backseat. "Warrick."

Wilber glanced in the rearview mirror, saying nothing. He didn't have to. It was Curt's fourth time kicking the thing over the past six hours. It had less to do with Curt having two left feet and more to do with the fact that Curt was hardly a small guy, but the crate was taking up valuable floor space in front of him.

Hugh grunted. "It's like you have a death wish."

"I once knew a guy with a death wish. We called him Deathwish Dexter. He won a bet and got one wish from Death. Not sure if he ever cashed in on it or not," said Petey as he rocked back and forth in his seat, staring out the window, seeming almost childlike in his enthusiasm. "Ironically enough, he's still alive, at least last I heard."

Jake flopped back on his seat. "That man once knew everyone."

Petey nodded as if he did actually once know everyone. "I'm hungry."

"You're fine," snapped Wilber. He'd lectured Petey at the roadside diner a few hours back about all the stops he was adding to the already long trip. They'd managed just over twenty-nine hours on the road over the course of three days on a trip that should have only taken twenty-six hours. And they weren't there yet. They still had another two hours to go. That wasn't exactly making great time. They'd thought the trip would take two days.

No one thought to factor in mishap after mishap. They'd had to deal with Hugh, Leo, and Jake's hugging, which ate up more time than one would think. The hotel they'd stayed at the first night had overbooked so they didn't have enough rooms. All the men had piled into one room with two queen beds and a sleeper sofa. Curt and Hugh had drawn the short straws and had to share the sleeper sofa.

The hugging potion hadn't been out of the man's system yet so that meant Curt got held most of the night by his best friend. It would have been mock-worthy if the same thing hadn't happened to Jake and Leo, who shared a bed at Wilber's demand. That had left Wilber on a bed all to himself and Petey in the van because he thought someone should guard it, even though the crate with the artifacts was in the hotel room.

As if that hadn't been enough, they'd gotten two flats through the second day of driving but had only had one spare. The van had overheated. Petey had to go to the bathroom every thirty minutes like clockwork. The motel they'd stayed in last night was questionable to say the least. But they had three rooms so no one had to share a bed.

They'd been on the road for almost six hours so far today. Curt was fairly sure the trip was cursed.

That or he was.

He paused, his hand going to his front pocket, where he still had the gold coin. He'd forgotten to give it to Wilber.

"I'm starving and I gotta go again," said Petey with a whine.

"Again?" asked Jake from the back. He turned, found the picnic basket his wife had sent. He opened it and pulled out various baked goods.

Curt shook his head, remembering all too well what Penelope and Kelsey had done already with baked goods. He did not want to suffer from uncontrollable urges to hug everyone. He'd leave that for the rest of them. "I'm good."

Hugh took the bags from Jake, said

nothing, but put them on the seat. He patted them gently as if knowing where they were might somehow make the fact he ate Petey's bathwater better.

"Do we know if this stuff is tainted with Petey's bathwater too?" asked Curt.

Hugh shook his head. "That's why it's staying right here."

"How about some tunes?" asked Petey before taking it upon himself to take over the sound system, if that's what it could be called, in the van.

In the next breath, "The Lion Sleeps Tonight" began to play, crackling somewhat, through the speakers.

Petey's eyes widened. "Warrick, you never told me someone wrote a song about you."

Hugh leaned forward and reached for the sound system.

Wilber swatted the man's hand.

Hugh grunted. "I'm not listening to this the rest of the trip. No way. No how."

"Everyone, sing along," said Petey, who belted out words to some song. Not the one playing.

Suddenly, Jake sat up straight and began to sing. The man's expression did not match the words coming out of his mouth. He looked scared as he grabbed his throat.

Leo, who had been napping next to Jake in the backseat, his feet up and against a window, raised his head and peeked out from one eye. He lifted a brow in his brother-in-law's direction.

Then, just like Jake, Leo began to sing along as well. He too looked stunned and confused.

He had a great voice.

When Hugh started singing as well, Curt sat up straight, accidentally kicking the crate once more. This time, he kicked it hard enough to pop the top open.

Petey played drums on the dashboard as Wilber pulled the van off the highway and down a side road. With no real sense of urgency, the older man parked the van off to the side of the road and then turned to face Petey.

"Tell them to stop singing," said Wilber, his voice flat.

Petey shook his head, rocking out to

some upbeat song about some Moonlight Bay. It had a vibe to it that made Curt think of songs from the early 1900s. The drumming that was still accompanying Petey's singing did not match the song in the least.

Wilber shut down the van's radio, but that did nothing to stop Petey from singing about Moonlight Bay or Hugh, Jake, and Leo to stop belting out about how the lion was sleeping that night.

Curt's gaze moved to the bags of baked goods on the seat next to him. He knew without asking that their current predicament had ties to the women and their cooking. "Uh-oh. Tell me this isn't a result of the potion. I would have thought that would be out of their system by now. Did the girls put it in everything they sent too?"

Wilber rubbed the bridge of his nose. "It gets worse."

"I'm almost afraid to ask how." Curt poked one of the bags like it contained poisonous snakes.

Wilber looked to Petey. "Petey, command them to sing the song you're singing. Make them sing 'Moonlight Bay.'"

With a shrug, Petey did as he was instructed.

The next Curt knew, the other men in the van began singing, as best they could considering no one knew the song, about Moonlight Bay.

Curt's eyes widened as he realized what Wilber had done. He'd just proven that whatever potion Petey had a hand in making left the man able to issue orders that had to be followed by those who ingested his dirty bathwater. Leaving Petey in charge of anything or anyone was a terrible idea.

"Yeah. That qualifies as worse," said Curt.

Wilber opened his van door.

"What are you doing?" asked Curt as the others kept singing. They were beginning to find a rhythm together and oddly started to sound like a barbershop quartet. In the interest of never letting a funny moment go by without documentation, Curt whipped out his phone and began recording.

If looks could kill, Curt would be six feet under from the expression Hugh gave him before yanking the phone from Curt's hand and pushing it out of the popped-open window.

Curt grinned at Petey. "Hey, Petey, how about you tell Hugh to pee on a fire hydrant?"

Petey stopped singing. "I've done that so many times I've lost count. It's never as fun as they make it out to be."

Wilber touched Petey's arm. "I cannot listen to this all the way down to Louisiana. Please make them stop."

Curt crawled over Hugh and opened the van door. He got out, stretched his legs, and then retrieved his cell phone.

Petey got out as well. "Gotta drain the lizard. I once knew a guy who actually tried to drain a lizard. Unfortunately for him the lizard he picked was really a were-gator and the were-gator didn't take kindly to the action. Pretty sure the draining guy was turned into a purse. Maybe boots. Can't remember. He was friends with the guy who blew up from holding in his wind, but he and the Dexter guy never got along."

Curt shook his head and was about to

find a tucked-away spot to join in the draining of lizards when he noticed something gold and shiny on the ground.

Strange.

He hadn't noticed it there only moments before when he'd picked up his phone. But there, bright as day, was the half-dollar-sized gold coin he'd had in his pocket. He bent, grabbed it and went to put it back in his pocket only to realize it wasn't the same coin. It just looked like it. The other was still in his pocket.

Confused, he turned the coin around in his hand, looking at the markings on it closer than he'd bothered to before. On one side was the head of a lion and on the other was a circle symbol he'd seen a few times around town. It was something he'd seen some of the witches wear on the ends of necklaces. A sign of magic or power. He wasn't totally sure. But he did know it wasn't a coincidence that another coin had turned up near him.

"Guys," he said, a sinking feeling coming over him. "Anyone know a lot about magic?"

"Leo does," said Petey.

Curt groaned. "Anyone who is not also a hunter?"

"What ya got there?" asked Petey, snatching the coin from Curt's hand. "Oh, shiny."

Curt watched the older man, painfully aware Petey had not washed his hands after his lizard draining. Thankfully, Curt had packed hand sanitizer in one of his bags.

Wilber whistled and put his hand out from the other side of the van.

Petey threw the coin directly to the hunter.

Wilber caught it and stiffened. "Warrick, where, exactly, did you find this?"

"Right here," said Curt, pointing down at the ground. "It's identical to the one Jake handed me before we left. Jake said I dropped that one and I tried to tell him it wasn't mine. This one was next to my foot."

"Kind of like that one?" asked Petey, motioning to the ground.

Curt looked down to find another gold coin there. He knew then and there something was up and he wasn't going to like it one bit.

Wilber leaned and put his head in through the open driver-side window. "Stop singing!"

The three men still in the van all looked out at Petey with wide eyes. They did not stop singing.

"Petey," said Curt.

Petey grumbled. "You suck the fun out of everything, Wilber. Fine. Stop singing!"

They stopped.

Jake was first out of the van. He charged in Petey's direction.

Curt headed him off. "Calm down."

"What was that? Why did I start singing? I do not sing." The centaur was anything but pleased.

Leo joined them. "Yeah. We noticed. You cannot carry a tune, Majoy. You can't work magic worth a damn either. What does my sister see in you? And we were singing because Petey commanded it. Looks like we found another side effect of his potion."

Sparks that were rainbow-colored shot

out of Jake's hands, indicating he was riled up.

Everyone backed up except Petey.

Curt grabbed the man by the suspenders and tugged, pulling him to safety. If Jake was going to burst into a rainbow of fruit flavors, it was best he not get it on everyone else.

Hugh got out of the van and ran his hands through his hair, aggravation pouring off him in waves. "Think happy thoughts so you don't end up bear-hugging Messing. Do not think about wringing Petey's neck. Do not think about wrapping your hands around his skinny little neck and...."

Wilber came around the side of the van, headed towards Curt just in time for Hugh to grab the man and hug him tight. Neither looked pleased by the events that were unfolding.

Petey smiled wide. "Get a picture of that, Warrick. Penelope will want to frame it and hang it on the wall."

"If you even so much as think about taking a picture, I'll have *your* pelt framed and hanging on *my* wall," warned Wilber, still in the process of being hugged tightly by the wolf-shifter.

Curt thought about it a second and decided to take his chances. He snapped a fast picture and was sure to quickly text it to Penelope.

Wilber grunted.

Hugh growled.

Petey clapped.

Jake nudged Curt. "Want to tell me why you're standing in the middle of what looks like spilled pirate treasure? Also, why were we singing?"

"I once knew a pirate," said Petey. "He had a big room full of gold pieces. Looked a lot like the ones Warrick has."

Curt tensed.

Petey looked him up and down slowly and then his eyes widened. "Warrick, are you really a pirate?"

"No. I'm not a pirate."

Petey walked around him slowly. "You sure? My pirate friend, Blackbeard, his gold coins can find their way to him if he summons them. You summoning them?"

Curt was about to answer Petey when

he realized what the old man had said. "You're claiming to have known Blackbeard, the famous pirate? Petey, you're old, I'll give you that, but I think Blackbeard died long before you were born."

"I never said I knew him when he was alive," added Petey with a wave of his hand as if Curt was the daft one.

Curt glanced down. There had to be around twenty gold coins at his feet. "Okay, I know those were not there before. What gives? Oo, am I a pirate?"

Wilber had to pry Hugh off him. When he was finally clear of the lovefest, he came for Curt and bent, lifting a few of the coins. His façade was even and unreadable.

Leo went to one knee and reached out, but right before the younger hunter would have made contact with a coin, he jerked his hand back and hissed.

"I'm right in assuming these are spelled?" asked Wilber of the other hunter.

"Oh yeah," said Leo, blowing on his fingertips. "Powerful magic."

Wilber lifted a coin to his mouth and licked it.

"Does it taste like chicken?" asked Petey.

Wilber groaned.

Curt held a coin in his hand. He blinked and more appeared around his feet.

Jake scratched the back of his head. "I want answers as to how it is Petey is able to give us orders we have to follow, but first, am I the only one who senses dark power on those coins?"

Leo stayed bent on one knee as he looked up at his brother-in-law. "It's not just you. They're coated in dark magic."

The same sinking feeling he'd felt before returned. "Wonderful. I'm a cursed pirate."

"You're not a pirate," said Wilber sternly.

"Warrick, who did you tick off this time? Who would want to curse you?" asked Hugh.

Petey rubbed his wiry jawline. "Probably every woman he's ever dated. I once was cursed by a woman I dated. She thought I was stepping out on her, but I wasn't. Dark powers had been at work, tricking lots of folks back then. Plus, her people didn't want her with me and my people didn't want me with her. It was a Romeo and Juliet kind of thing. When my girl's temper flared, out popped the curse. Let me tell you, it's no fun to carry that black cloud around with you. Truth be told, it's why I didn't stay down in Hedgewitch Cove."

Curt opened his mouth to argue as much but realized the older man was correct. The odds of the curse coming from a woman he'd upset was high. He wasn't the type of guy who committed to any one woman. He never made any bones about it. He was upfront with the women he dated, letting them know that if they were looking for a future or long-term, they were meowing up the wrong tree. This cat-shifter wanted to live all nine of his lives free from restrictions.

The type of women he went for normally seemed fine with his proclamation that he wasn't in it for something real. They were as shallow as he was, if not more. He preferred it that way. He liked women who drove fast cars, wore tight dresses, and who were always in high heels. There was nothing quite like a hot chick in pumps.

His body tightened just thinking about it.

Oh yes, he had a type and that type tended to go into dating him with their eyes wide open. Besides, most of the women he selected had no interest in something real or more. They were living for the moment too. Though there had been a few he suspected said as much but did not truly mean it. And then there were the ones who thought he'd call them for second dates.

He never did.

That wasn't really his style.

"If we're counting women I've dated the list is going to be too long for me to state or remember. I could narrow it to the ones I've managed to get mad at me, but that won't actually shave many names off the list," said Curt honestly.

Jake shook his head. "Let me phrase it this way. Who would want to curse you bad enough to make it happen when you're how many hours from Everlasting? A spell that can reach you this far from home, while you're traveling, is a big one. That takes some power right there."

Wilber stood and began handing Curt the gold coins.

"I don't want them," said Curt, trying to give them back to the hunter.

He refused to take them.

"Isn't part of your job to watch over magical items?" asked Curt with a grunt.

Wilber snorted. "Son, my job is not to clean up after your relationship messes. And to think I wanted my granddaughter mated to you, not the heathen."

Hugh grinned. "He's making me look like the better choice now, isn't he, Gramps?"

"Never mind," snapped Wilber. "The cursed lion-shifter who secretly wants to be a pirate is still winning."

Hugh went for the man and bear-hugged him again. "That was a gift from me to you. No dirty bathwater needed. Admit it. I'm growing on you."

Wilber shoved Hugh away and groaned.

Leo stood slowly and nodded to the

coins in Curt's hands. "Drop them. They're spelled with chaos."

Curt couldn't have let go of them faster if he tried. "I'm not going to start wanting to hug everyone or sing showtunes or anything, am I? My man bits aren't about to fall off, are they?"

He cupped himself.

Hugh looked at Leo. "Wait. This spell of chaos thing you said. Would that explain everything that has gone wrong on this trip so far?"

Leo nodded. "Oh yeah. It would totally explain it all. It would also mean we're far from out of the woods."

Hugh gave Curt a hard look. "Warrick."

"Hey, do not blame me."

Leo cracked his knuckles. "I vote we leave the cat-shifter here and go on without him."

Hugh shook his head. "No. The cursed cat-shifter is coming with us."

"Thanks," said Curt.

Petey bent and picked up a coin. When he turned it over the symbol on it was different than the others. It was a triple moon. "I've seen this before. It was used in the spell that broke apart me and my girl. It's nasty magic. Dark."

Wilber took another look at one of the coins and his jaw set. "Warrick, who did you upset enough to want you dead? The rest of those may be spelled with chaos, but this one here, it's the mark of death."

"What?" asked Curt, stepping back. "Someone wants to kill me?"

"Not that shocking," said Hugh. "I'm also second-guessing letting you ride with us the rest of the way. The weird hunter-guy-who-lives-in-the-army-jacket might be on to something."

Leo ignored the dig.

Wilber looked at him and Hugh shut up. "So who wants you dead, Warrick?"

Cursing him with some bad luck or whatever was one thing; cursing him to death was something altogether different. "No one. Okay, Hugh, but he only pretends to want to kill me all the time. He wouldn't really do it."

"True," said Hugh. He then leveled a

hard gaze on Curt. "Hell hath no fury like a woman—"

"I once knew a Fury. She was a real looker," said Petey. "If she yelled, all the glass in the area would break. That was problematic. She was dating a leprechaun and let me tell you, those leprechauns may be lookers, but they sure know how to make a woman mad. Got so bad the town voted and decided the two could no longer be a couple. She packed up and left town. Not sure what happened to the leprechaun. He worked at the bank there. Ironic. I know."

Curt took a small step back and stepped on more coins. He went to shove his phone into his back pocket only to find a coin there too. With a gasp he tossed it far from him only to find more coins appearing in his pockets.

He threw them all, yet more continued to appear as if there was a never-ending magical source of them.

Petey grinned. "Warrick is making change."

"Uh, guys?" asked Jake, something off in his voice.

"What?" snapped Wilber.

Jake pointed to the van. "Is it supposed to glow?"

They turned to find the van engulfed in a ball of blinding white light. Wilber spun around and cuffed the back of Curt's ear. "You and your big feet!"

Hugh grunted. "Warrick, if your bad luck just started the end of the world, I'm going to kill you myself and save the female population the time!"

"I once knew a guy who tried to end the world," said Petey.

Chapter Six

MISSI PEDALED her bike through the tiny streets of Hedgewitch Cove, in the direction of the restaurant. Riding a bike in a long skirt wasn't easy, but Missi had perfected the art. She also rode around wearing flip-flops (when she remembered shoes). She rode harder up the slight incline of the street. Because she rode her bike, affectionately named Shirley, everywhere she never lacked for daily exercise.

Mr. Flanks was walking on the sidewalk, near the shaved iced stand. He waved. The older gentleman was in a tweed sports coat, despite it being hot and humid, a red bowtie, a white dress shirt, and a pair of brown slacks. His wingtip shoes were polished and looking their best, as was always the case with the man. He had a head full of stark white hair that was cut close. He kept a white moustache that worked well for him. Looking at him, one would think he was a normal, everyday Southern older gentleman. They'd never assume he came from a long line of witches himself (even if that line of witches had once had ties to dark magic) and was one of the most sought-after cauldron makers in the South. "Mornin', Mississippi."

She didn't really have time to stop, but it wasn't in her to be rude. And she did need to speak with the man about his upcoming fall cauldron collection. He, unlike Beatrice, did not run his business out of the back of his home. No. Mr. Flanks had a small factory on the edge of town. It made an assortment of cast-iron products, cauldrons being one of them.

She stopped the bike and stood, keeping the bicycle balanced between her legs. "Mr. Flanks, how are you this morning?"

"Right as rain," he said before thumbing towards Shiver Me Timbers Shaved Iced Stand. It was a favorite spot during the hot Louisiana summer days.

Missi noticed the stand wasn't open yet. That was odd. "Blackbeard hasn't opened the stand yet?"

Blackbeard—the infamous pirate who was now a spirit but appeared very much alive to those around him—had called Hedgewitch Cove home since before it was even a town. He often told pirate stories about the waters off the coast of Louisiana. He talked about the glory days and his rivalries, as well as treasures he'd acquired throughout his time sailing the seas.

His shaved iced stand always, on operating days, had a line by noon, well into the evening. Mr. Flanks had never been a fan of the stand. He thought the business cheapened the overall image of the town and that something more respectable than a shaved ice stand needed to be there.

More than once the two had argued about it. If Ms. Cherry was right, the pair had been at it again the other night.

The stand was normally open by now and with the Founder's Day activities around the corner, Blackbeard had been offering extended hours. The only time she could recall his stand not opening when it was supposed to had been when Missi was in high school and some of the upperclassmen decided their senior prank would be capturing Blackbeard and trapping the man in a bottle. It was their play on a ship in a bottle, but with a pirate in the bottle. Her brother York had been one of the teens and Blackbeard had never forgotten or forgiven him. It turns out when you're a ghost and vanquished to a bottle, you show up in there minus clothing. Then you're a naked ghost in a bottle. And when you're freed, you're a naked ghost outside of a bottle.

Blackbeard was not a man you wanted upset with you. He hadn't become notorious as a pirate for nothing. And he'd not done so by sheer luck. He too had magic in his bloodline. It was part of the reason his spirit differed from many others in the fact he appeared to be very much alive. You could touch him. He was warm, and very handsome.

Very.

Very handsome.

The painting and pictures she'd seen in books that were supposed to represent his likeness looked nothing like him. She'd asked him about them once and he'd laughed and told her he had his first mate pretend to be him often to keep suspicion off him.

Blackbeard was like any other man in town. He ate, drank, and needed sleep. The only thing he couldn't do was leave the town limits. Not if he wanted to keep his corporeal form. She'd never seen him go beyond Hedgewitch Cove limits, but she knew he'd done it at least once. That was how her brother and the others had been able to capture him in a bottle years ago.

Missi closed her eyes a moment. "I really hope York didn't ..."

Mr. Flanks glanced back at the stand. "I'm not sure why he isn't open. So, what has you out and about this mornin'?"

"I'm doing a favor for Virginia," she

said. "While I have you, can you get me information on your upcoming fall line?"

He nodded. "Of course. I should have brochures in by next week. I'll drop one by."

"Thank you."

He glanced back at the stand and then rubbed his cheek. "You best be on your way now. You take care of yourself, Mississippi. Don't you be lettin' York turn you into a wild child like him."

She hid her smile. "I won't, sir."

She continued, hoping to get to the restaurant before the magic that kept humans from seeing the truth about the town wore off. The average timeframe was an hour. If the human was weak-willed it would last for several hours. If they were stubborn, it was less. Then there was the rare occasion when it didn't work at all.

She peddled through the stop sign, feeling like a law breaker for not stopping, but there simply wasn't time. Runes Restaurant & Pub had an amazing spot, right on the water. But that meant it was a decent ride from her shop. As she turned the corner she could see the delivery truck down the road a ways, parked out in front of Runes. The establishment dated back generations. It was a staple of the town. The tourists who visited, who were all supernatural, raved about it on various review websites.

Just then she noticed Furfur running down the center of Water Street with a human bone in his mouth. It was a femur if Missi wasn't mistaken. She sucked in a big breath, hoping the delivery man was still under the influence of the spell. She also hoped someone noticed Furfur had clearly been digging at the cemetery again. Poor Luc would catch Hell over it. Not that he'd mind, being the devil and all.

Missi rode faster and nearly collided with the parked truck in her hurry. She propped her bicycle against the building and ran around to the side door. There she found a tall, plump man, with a sizable belly that looked ready to pop a button on his dark blue work shirt.

He cast her an annoyed look. "You Virginia?"

She shook her head and withdrew her set of keys. With the number of businesses her family ran, her key ring was full. She dropped it and the man sighed as she retrieved it. "No, sir. I'm Mississippi."

He huffed. "Virginia? Mississippi? Some names you got there."

She cast an artificial smile as she found the correct key and disengaged the lock. "My parents used to travel around the United States in an RV. My siblings and me are named after the state we were either conceived or born in. Just depends."

He glanced around. "Folks in this town are a might odd."

"You don't know the half of it," she mumbled, opening the door and stepping back so he could move his dolly full of boxes in. She followed as he unloaded the boxes. She wrung her hands, wanting him to go sooner rather than later. She'd gotten lucky with Furfur. There was no way she could explain Headless Hank if the man saw the barber jogging.

Minutes ticked by as the man brought in six more dolly-loads full of boxes before presenting her with a paper to sign. She did and then practically shoved him towards the door. "Looks like rain. You should get a move on."

"It's clear as can be," he protested.

She motioned to the door and then gave him a tiny push with her power. It wasn't something she liked doing because it was technically considered dark magic. When she spoke, her voice held a level of power that would make a human want to obey. "It looks like rain. It's best you head out of Hedgewitch Cove now."

He nodded and glanced up to stare at the sky, just as a tall, buff, headless male body wearing a red tracksuit jogged past. "Hmm, looks like rain. I should head out now."

Missi held her breath and didn't exhale until the delivery man was in his truck and driving away. She then turned and stormed back into the restaurant. Virginia owed her big time. Once inside she tried to call her sister, but Virginia's cell went to voicemail.

"Crisis averted. Barely. I just hope he got out of town before the spell wore off. I'll expect you to donate a kidney should I have need of one."

Missi glanced out of the front window and spotted Barnebas Cybulski on his daily route, a post office bag slung over one shoulder while he sorted mail and walked. The man took his position very seriously. So much so that he'd made her life something of a living hell with his attempts to acquire her back lot in order to expand the post office.

She wondered if Jasmine had cornered him and told him of the new foe he'd face for the lot. Not that she was selling to anyone. It was hers and she wasn't about to part with it.

Barnebas came to a stop just outside of the gated front entrance of Hells Gate Inn. The small, quaint inn was owned by Luc Dark. Since it really did house a portal to hell in it, he'd themed the inn accordingly.

Missi couldn't help but smile as she watched the mailman unlatch the iron gate with great care and slowness, as if doing so might not alert the undead or demons within. He then began to tiptoe up the walk path towards the wraparound porch.

By step four, his bag lifted of its own accord, mail flew up and out of it, scattering about in a small, self-contained tornado happening just above Barnebas's head, and Furfur, who called the inn home, charged into the yard, still carrying a human femur in his mouth.

Barnebas's eyes widened and his shouts could be heard from her spot as he grabbed for the swirling mail, tried to hold down his bag, and took off running towards the gate once more.

A relative newcomer to the town, Sigmund Bails, opened the front door of the inn and walked out without a care in the world, or a shirt on.

Missi froze, admiring the view. More than once she, Virginia, Beatrice, and Jasmine had gone to the docks with chairs and a picnic lunch to watch as Sigmund worked on one of York's fishing boats. The men tended to get hot and take their shirts off during the day. While the sight of York without a shirt did nothing for her, it seemed to please Jasmine and other women who also just happened to be in the area then as well. Sometimes Blackbeard joined in and that made it even better.

Sigmund ignored the flying mail and the hellhound with a bone in its mouth. She wondered what the town he was from was like if he didn't think much of the common occurrences of Hedgewitch Cove.

Sigmund went to the gate and calmly put out his hand. Barnebas placed mail in it and stood there, waiting as Sigmund walked back towards the swirling mail and shook his head, looking more tired than scared.

The mail instantly fell neatly into a pile in Sigmund's hand. He then returned it to Barnebas and inclined his head, pushing his glasses up as he did. The man was handsome and screamed bookworm. She wasn't sure how he managed to pull it off, but he did.

With a slight laugh, Missi watched Barnebas lift a fist and shake it towards the attic window of the inn, shouting something about ruing the day to one of the spirits. The man would never learn. Taunting them only gave them attention—something they were desperate for.

Chapter Seven

"HMM, DOESN'T LOOK THE SAME," said Petey as Curt drove Sunshine into Hedgewitch Cove. "For starters it didn't have paved roads. This was a dirt road back in my day."

The sign announcing their arrival was made of planks of wood with carved, ornate letters and the year it was established. The craftsmanship was impressive and oddly familiar. It reminded him of Hugh's woodworking, but that couldn't be. Hugh had never made a sign for the town. Curt was always in and out of Hugh's garage, which was where the man made all kinds of things. Curt would have noticed a sign for a town, especially with the sheer size of the sign. Besides, this one looked well-kept but aged, as if it had been there a very long time. Someone kept up on painting the raised portions of the letters. A well-tended flower bed was at the base of it and large oak trees dotted the backdrop.

Curt had to admit it was a picturesque welcoming. That was good. If he did end up liking the property he was set to view, he could play off the same look of the sign. Tourists would eat it up.

As they got closer to the sign, Curt noticed initials at the bottom right corner of it. He'd seen those initials, carved just like that before. "Petey, did you have something to do with that sign?"

Petey squirmed in his seat, appearing uncomfortable with the question. He then nodded. "My girl wanted a sign for the town. I made her one."

"Your girl?" asked Curt, intrigued. "Want to tell me more about this mystery woman who stole your heart before a certain witch back in Everlasting did?"

Petey put his hands on his knees and

stared out at the sign as they drove by. It was evident the man wasn't comfortable with the subject. Petey reached under his seat and pulled out a flask. Before Curt could lecture him about having an open container in the vehicle, the man was taking a swig. "Not much to tell," said Petey before wiping the back of his mouth with his hand and capping the flask. "Dark magic came between us and once that was sorted, it was too late. She'd started a life with another man. For the best. I'm a free spirit. Can't hold me down."

His tone and forlorn expression spoke otherwise.

Hugh patted Petey's arm from the backseat. "Everlasting's win. Hedgewitch Cove's loss."

"That's right," Curt said just as he hit a pothole. The entire van bounced.

Everyone held their breath as Curt got it under control. They were less worried about the pothole and more worried about the reason Curt was driving and Wilber wasn't.

When Curt had kicked the crate by

accident, he'd broken one of the artifacts within it. They'd learned as much when Wilber and Leo had finally managed to get the massive white light that had engulfed the van to subside.

Curt glanced in the rearview mirror to find Wilber sitting next to Hugh, holding a broken artifact on his lap, giving Curt the stink-eye. The retired hunter had been doing as much since the bright light thing that apparently, could have ended the world. "Doesn't know how to sit still and can't drive worth a damn."

"I wasn't aiming at the pothole," offered Curt.

"Could have fooled me."

"I told you I'd drive," snapped Hugh at Wilber.

"I'd rather take my chances with the cursed cat-shifter at the wheel," returned Wilber.

Petey bent and came up with another gold coin. "Warrick, this just fell out of your pocket. You're making change again."

Curt groaned.

Wilber snorted. "I'm starting to see why

someone marked you with a spell of chaos and a death note."

Curt swallowed hard. "I already said I was sorry for kicking the crate."

"Well then. All is forgiven," said Wilber. "Nearly ending the world is no big deal. A quick sorry should fix it. You and your big feet."

"I'm cursed," said Curt with an innocent grin.

"Likely excuse," replied Wilber.

"I once knew a guy who nearly ended the world," said Petey, earning him groans from everyone in the van. "It's true. He's done it more than once. It's sort of his thing. Real doom and gloomer, always thinking the end is near. We called him Apocalypse Arnold."

Curt ignored Petey and looked out at the town of Hedgewitch Cove. It seemed like the South's version of Everlasting, with its tree-lined streets. Small, well-kept homes were on both sides of the road as they slowed to obey the speed limit. There were sidewalks, and streetlamps that looked to be gas lit were spaced evenly on each side of the two-lane street. Side streets had streetlamps with actual street signs on them as well, much like the ones he remembered seeing in the French Quarter the last time he'd been to New Orleans.

In fact, Hedgewitch Cove seemed a lot like Everlasting and the French Quarter got together and spit out a lovechild.

The trees on both sides of the street bathed the road in shade, helping to block some of the hot Louisiana sun. It was still relatively early in the day, but it was certainly humid. Much more so than Maine ever was. In fact, compared to Hedgewitch Cove, Maine didn't even have humidity.

"Petey, I'm starting to see why you run around in a knit cap all year round," said Curt. "If you were used to this heat, Everlasting has to feel frigid to you."

Petey nodded. "When I first went back up north, I thought certain parts of me were gonna freeze right off. I'm used to the cold now. But it's nice when Hugh takes me down to Florida during the coldest months."

"Sorry we didn't make it down this

year," said Hugh. "I told you that you're welcome to go down and use the house there anytime you want. You can live there all the time if you want."

Petey pressed a smile to his face. "Thanks."

Curt had a feeling Petey would brave any amount of cold if it meant he could stay near the people he thought of as family.

Jake sat up in the far backseat. "Check out the purple house. Polly would love it."

Off to the right was a small home with a shaded porch. It had a high pitch roof and the wood of the home was painted a light purple. Huge dark purple shutters flanked each window, extending from the porch floor to the ceiling. They looked heavily used, yet cared for. Large potted ferns hung from baskets across the front of the porch.

Two cats sat on the porch, watching the van as the men drove by. One cat was black with a white bowtie mark on his breast. The other was white with a black bowtie mark.

Both cats didn't take their gaze from the men.

Leo grunted. "Those cats are giving me the willies."

Petey nodded. "As they should. If I'm right, they belong to a Corduas witch." He shuddered. "Bad news. They've had familiars that look like that for hundreds of years. Might even be the same ones. I never did get too close to them to figure it out."

"We talking Babcock level of bad news?" asked Leo.

As Everlasting had recently had issues with its own line of bad witches popping up causing trouble, all the men were familiar with dark magic.

Petey glanced back at Wilber, and Curt wondered how much the old hunter knew about Petey's past. Knowing Wilber, he knew everything. "They'd not eaten anyone that I know of, but they're power hungry. And they caused a lot of chaos before I left town."

"I'm told that's behind them," said Wilber. "But one never can tell."

"That true of former hunters?" asked

Hugh, blinking innocently at his grandfather-in-law.

Wilber leveled a murderous gaze upon the wolf-shifter. "Let's find out."

Curt glanced in the rearview mirror again. "Don't make us force some of those cookies down you."

Wilber actually cracked a smile.

"Anything looking familiar to you yet, Petey?" asked Curt as they continued to drive slowly through the town. A sign for Flanks Ironworks was off to the right, near a side street. The sign, like everything else so far, fit the vibe of the town.

"Medusa's Cavern?" asked Hugh, looking off to a sign on the left.

"Hair salon," said Jake, reminding everyone he'd spent a good deal of time in the town.

"Really?" asked Hugh.

Jake nodded. "If we're in town long enough, you have to stop by the barber shop. Trust me when I say it's an experience *all* unto itself."

Petey grinned. "That it is. Hank is a hell of a barber."

"Jake, where is the realtor's office? I'm supposed to meet up with some woman who is going to show me available properties." Curt slowed as he saw a child kicking a ball in the front lawn of one of the homes. He drove past at a snail's pace, wanting to be safe rather than sorry should the ball get away from the child and it dart into the street.

"It's on Pearl Street. I'll take you by after we get settled in at the Inn," said Jake. "You thinking of opening a restaurant down here? They have a lot of food places as it is."

"The South does food right," said Leo, patting his nonexistent gut. "They fry just about anything."

Hugh grinned. "My kind of people. My wife likes to try to force healthy choices on me."

"And Petey's dirty bathwater," added Wilber with a snort.

Hugh grunted.

Curt could see signs of businesses up ahead. As they approached, the size of the homes increased as well. Some were massive. And all of them looked as if they were ready to be photographed for a magazine cover or have a painting done of the area. Curt had always thought Everlasting went out of its way to be presentable, but Hedgewitch Cove looked to have written the book on the matter.

A large banner was strung across the street, high in the air. It announced a month full of Founder's Day activities and celebrations. He snorted. "Petey, did they roll out a welcome wagon for you?"

He'd meant it as a joke since Petey was so old.

When Petey glanced at him and sighed, Curt stiffened. "I was a founder myself. Helped to name the town and everything."

It was then Curt realized something big had to have gone down for Petey to have walked away from it all. He didn't pry, but he wanted to.

"Curt, go on up past the big circular magic shop there and then, a few blocks down, when you get to the stop sign, make a right," said Jake from the far back.

Sure enough, there was a huge circular

building just past a rather large lot that only had what looked to be a garden on it. Curt wondered if that was the lot the realtor had told him could possibly be purchased because of a loophole in the town charter. It was a great location, close to downtown, which looked to be the heart of the town.

The magic shop's building had a few things left to be desired. It was big, dark red, and had crystals hanging all around it from the edge of the roof. That would have to go.

"The Inn will be down Water Street a bit on the right. It's right across the street from the water. Has a great view. Sig's room has one of the best views in the place. Can't miss it," said Jake. "Luc is showy like that. Wait until you meet Furfur. He's got a thing about chasing cats. Saw him running from a parrot though. Strange beast."

"Furfur as in the demon who commands legions in hell?" asked Curt.

Wilber made a strange noise indicating surprise.

Curt snorted. "Hey, I know things."

Jake laughed. "Yes. But trust me when I say you'd never know it was one in the same looking at him. Luc has an odd sense of humor."

Curt still had a hard time believing Luc Dark owned an inn in Hedgewitch Cove. He'd never mentioned anything to Curt or Hugh about it before and they had lunch with him once a month when he was in Everlasting. They were aware he hung his hat in more than one location. They just hadn't known Hedgewitch Cove was one of them. Guess being the devil meant you had to spread yourself around.

"Anyone let Sig know we're coming?" asked Curt.

Jake shook his head, as did Hugh.

"No. And I asked Jolene not to say anything," said Wilber. "Figured the boy could use the surprise."

Boy?

Hardly.

He was in his early thirties, just like Hugh and Curt.

"Are you and Jolene an item?" asked Jake of Wilber.

The question earned the centaur a slow, heavy stare from Wilber.

Jake put his hands up. "Sorry I asked."

"So are you?" asked Hugh, seemingly unconcerned with how much he irritated Wilber. There had been a time, not that long ago, when Hugh had been downright terrified of the man. A lot had changed since October.

Petey went for the radio again (making it his sixth attempt since Curt had taken over driving). This time he managed to get it to play. The entire van filled with the sounds of "The Lion Sleeps Tonight" again. Apparently, it was the only song the damn van played. Curt tried to shut it off again but ended up in a slapping match with the older man. Somehow, Petey won.

"Ouch!" yelled Curt as Petey bit him in the hand. Curt stared wide-eyed at the man. "I'm going to need to get my shots updated now."

"Brake first. Shots later," said Petey.

Hugh sat up fast and grabbed Curt's shoulder roughly. "Stop the van, Curt!"

Curt slammed on the brakes and Sunshine came to a screeching halt. Suddenly, the inside of the van sounded as if someone had won at the slot machines in Vegas. The clinking of falling coins was loud.

Curt glanced down at the floor of the van to find the driver-side floor covered in gold coins.

Petey pointed at them. "Jackpot!"

Slowly, Curt pulled his gaze from the floor of the van up and out the front window.

Abruptly, it felt as if someone had dropped a ton of bricks on him instead of a ton of cursed coins.

The air swooshed from his lungs as he took in the beautiful vision standing in front of the van. Long, dark waves of hair hung down to the woman's shapely waist. She wore a peasant shirt that was off-white and cut low enough for him to see the tops of her breasts.

His throat went dry.

Desperate for something to quench his thirst, he reached out in Petey's direction. The old man shoved the flask into Curt's hand. Thankfully, it was empty, or Curt might have been tempted to drink it.

Huge chocolate brown eyes stared at him from behind thick black lashes. The woman's skin was tanned and looked as if it might be that way year-round. Her lips were puckered in a way that said she was surprised.

Curt couldn't see all of her as the front of the van eclipsed most of her but from what he could see she looked a lot like she'd stepped right out of the sixties and into his sexiest dreams. He'd never before found himself attracted to a woman who wasn't dressed in a tight, expensive dress and wearing bright red lipstick. And he'd never ever been this attracted to one ever, no matter what she was wearing. The woman in front of the van didn't look to have on any makeup. The tiniest of freckles dotted the top of her nose and upper cheeks. If one wasn't staring hard at her, they'd have missed them.

His entire body lit with need and became very aware of the woman. Gulping, he suddenly wished the van had air conditioning because it seemed to be extra hot in the thing all of a sudden. He tugged at his collared short-sleeved shirt and actually entertained removing it to help cool his body. He wasn't the type of guy who made a habit of taking his clothes off in public.

"Is it me or is Warrick about to hump the steering wheel?" asked Hugh.

"Classy," snapped Wilber.

"Just calling it like I see it," said Hugh.

Ignoring Hugh, Curt watched as the woman's brown gaze narrowed and her jaw set. Anger rolled off her in such a way that even Hugh, the king of angry looks, would be impressed. As he realized just how close she was to the front end of the van, his chest tightened. He'd nearly run her over. A line of curses escaped his lips. He shocked himself with them.

"Someone give him a cookie," snapped Hugh. "He needs hugs and better word choices."

"Being mated has really tamed you, Lupine," said Petey.

"The word you're looking for is neutered," said Wilber.

Jake laughed and then shut up fast,

evidently realizing he was in the same boat as Hugh.

Petey laughed. "She looks like she wants to shove her sunflower up his whoops-a-daisy."

"I really hope she does," quipped Wilber.

"You are all so weird," added Leo.

"You get used to it," interjected Jake.

Leo sighed. "That's what I'm afraid of."

Petey pointed at the woman. "The look on her face says she's madder than a wet hen, Warrick."

The man was right. She did look good and angry.

The woman slapped the front of the van and then pointed at Curt. "You went right through the stop sign. You didn't so much as slow down. You could have killed someone! Are you drinking?"

Drinking?

Petey nudged the hand Curt held the flask in. Curt opened his mouth to object, but the woman kept on yelling at him. He just sat there, behind the wheel, holding a flask from which he had not taken a sip, with cursed gold coins littering the floor around him, a broken, possibly world-ending artifact being held together in the seat behind him, and a dumbfounded look upon his face.

He dropped the flask. That didn't seem to make any of it better.

Currently, he was about as far from winning at life as one could get. That being said, he really did feel like he'd won something as he stared at the irate woman. She was a prize indeed. His lion stirred and peeked up, confirming what the man already knew—she was special.

"Jackpot," he whispered.

Petey snorted.

"Warrick, she looks like she wants to castrate you," said Hugh.

"Best kind of woman," added Petey. "They keep a man on his toes. Hold up. There is something familiar about her."

"Well, do you have anything to say for yourself? I've got a mind to come up in there and tan your hide," the woman declared as she looked over the van. A confused expression came over her face.

"What in the world are you driving? Ohmygoddess! Run over by flower power? No. Not happening. No way. No how. Absolutely not!"

She paled.

Curt just kept staring at her without saying anything. Right now, his brain and his man parts were having issues thinking clearly. Pretty much the only thing his brain was able to come up with was "hot chick." And that was on loop.

His lion was pushing at him from within, doing its best to convince him that now would be a great time to let it free to do as it pleased. From its sense of urgency, it wanted the woman before him.

Mine.

The thought jarred him.

The woman slapped the front of the van again. "A curse on mating and a curse on you!"

Just like that, Curt found a bunch of coins falling on his head, coming out of thin air. They clunked and clanged, pelting him hard enough so that he actually yelped once.

They filled his lap, spilled off it and onto the floor around him. He looked and felt like something from a cartoon. At any moment a coyote might happen by with a stick of dynamite or an anvil might fall on his head.

It was that ludicrous.

When the coins were done raining down on him, Petey leaned, picked one up and wheezed. "Huh, another one that means death. Wow. Warrick, you really are cursed. But from the looks of you, you already know as much. Boy, you're sweatin' like a sinner in church."

The temperature in the van rose more as Curt continued to stare at the woman. He couldn't be sure, but it seemed like she was getting more and more attractive with each passing minute.

It took Curt a moment to realize someone was laughing hysterically behind him. He turned around slowly to find Wilber bent forward, hugging the broken artifact to him as he cackled. Curt couldn't recall a time in his life that he'd ever seen Wilber laugh so hard. It was probably for the best. The man looked downright psychotic.

Hugh inched away from him on the seat, his eyes wide. "That in *no* way is disconcerting."

Jake snorted. "I told you he was crazy."

"You're just mad he got the jump on you and tied you to a chair," added Leo.

Jake snarled softly. "Really love bonding with you, brother-in-law."

"Yeah. It's peachy," returned Leo.

Petey rocked back and forth in his seat, looking like an excited child who had just been told they were about to head to a circus. "Penelope and Kelsey were right. This trip has been fun! Curt, try going to the bathroom. I want to see if coins fall out of your…"

"Petey," warned Hugh.

Curt sat fixated on the woman in front of the van. Reaching out, he gripped the wheel, white-knuckling it, wanting to touch her.

Mine.

He stiffened.

"Oh my word, child, are you all right?"

asked an older gentleman in a tweed jacket as he hurried out and into the street and touched the woman's arm. "I saw the whole thing. He nearly killed you."

Curt swallowed hard.

The woman glared up at Curt. "I'm so mad I could spit."

He wasn't exactly sure how that equaled being mad, but from the sound of her voice, it wasn't a good thing.

Petey whistled low and shook his head. "You've gone and stepped in it."

The woman continued to glare at Curt. "Cat got your tongue?"

Petey rubbed his temple. "Since you're a lion-shifter, does that mean the cat has all of you? Not just your tongue?"

Hugh laughed. "I like her."

"Me too," said Curt, still gripping the wheel, staring dumbfounded out at the woman. He normally had far more game than he was presenting. "Can I keep her?"

Wilber kicked the back of the driver's seat. "You're starting to make Lupine look like a catch."

Hugh snorted. "Thanks."

Curt's focus returned to the woman in front of the van. She couldn't have been more than five-six but the look on her face made her seem like a giant. Curt applied the parking brake and shut off the van before getting out of it slowly. Coins fell out and onto the road as he did. He ignored them and looked at the woman. "I'm so sorry, miss. I was trying to get Petey to stop playing the lion song, then he bit me, and the next I knew, you were there."

Her gaze narrowed on him and he realized just how amazing her eyes were. A man could get lost in them. "So you nearly killed me over a song?"

"No," he said quickly before thinking harder about it. "Erm, yes."

The older gentleman with her looked Curt up and down. "Shifters. The lot of you are impossible to deal with. I can't believe they give your kind driver's licenses. I once knew a wolf-shifter who drove a truck straight through…"

"Ned Flanks? Is that you?" asked Petey, hurrying out of the van.

The man in the tweed jacket regarded

Don't Stop Bewitching

Petey, appearing confused. "Do I know you?"

Petey licked his palm and tried to smooth the bits of hair sticking out from his knit cap. "It's me. Captain Peter."

Peter?

Ned jerked back. "Peter, what in Sam Hill happened to you? You were always rough around the edges, but not like this."

Curt focused on the woman. "I'm sorry. Really. I am."

She glanced briefly at him and then touched Petey's arm lightly. "Excuse me, sir, but you wouldn't happen to be Captain Petey, would you?"

Petey faced her and stilled. "Who is asking? I don't know your mother, do I? I don't think I have any children out there, but you never can be too sure at my age and with how good I am with the ladies."

Curt groaned.

The woman surprised him by smiling wide. "You know my grandmother, or Mémé Marie-Claire as she likes to be called."

Petey stared at her and then gasped.

"Marie-Claire Caillat? I don't know why I didn't see it straight away. You look a lot like her. Is she still here in Hedgewitch Cove?"

"She's still in town. She's mentioned you more than once," said the woman. "Apparently, you're the one that got away."

Petey blushed. "She happy?"

The woman watched him for a moment. "If you're asking if she's still married, the answer is no. I don't know the details of it all, but I can tell you that my grandfather hasn't been in the picture since long before I was born. Apparently, there was a falling-out of some sort. My family doesn't discuss it. So she's single and, like I said, talks about you a lot."

Curt stepped back, sure he'd heard that wrong. There was no way anyone considered Petey the one that got away.

"Mississippi, are you all right?" asked Ned.

Mississippi.

That was certainly an interesting name.

In an instant Curt remembered what Penelope and Kelsey had told him before he'd left. They'd said the crystal ball had shown them a map of the state of Mississippi when they'd asked it about his mate.

He gulped.

No.

It couldn't be.

She wasn't his mate.

Was she?

Chapter Eight

HYPERVENTILATING SEEMED like a really good plan. Curt nearly went with it as his mind raced with what Penelope and Kelsey had told him they'd seen in regards to his mate.

The man in the tweed jacket stayed close to Mississippi. "Did he hit you with the van or just the bike?"

"I'm fine, no thanks to Mr. Flashy," she said, glancing at Curt.

He was at a loss for words.

"Warrick, I'm holding the fate of the world in my hands and you have a curse on your head!" shouted Wilber from inside the van. "Ask the young lady to dinner and then get your butt back in here. We need to get to Hells Gate."

She tipped her head. "Curt Warrick?"

Curt offered a sexy smile. Now they were getting somewhere. He knew he had more skills with the ladies than were showing. "Yes. Heard about me?"

She snorted. "Oh yeah. Sigmund talks about you. Says you have more money than you know what to do with and that you're kind of full of yourself. Just what we needed, another rich guy in town."

Hugh opened the van door. "Sig isn't wrong. Okay, Curt. The nice young woman doesn't like you and she's known you thirty seconds. Now that we've established she's a good judge of character, get in here and drive us to Luc's before Wilber lets go of the doomsday device here and hugging each other is the least of our worries."

"Hugging each other?" asked Mississippi.

Curt licked his lips. "It's a long story."

Petey beamed. "I fed 'em my dirty bathwater and now they won't stop hanging on each other. Hugh held Warrick all night. I got a picture of it on my phone if you want to see it. Sent it to Hugh's wife already. Got me a good one of Leo and Jake too. Kelsey has a copy of it now."

Mississippi looked downward and then stiffened. Her gaze snapped up and on to him. "You broke Shirley!"

"Shirley?" he asked, fearing he'd actually hit and killed someone.

She pointed down.

Petey bent and yanked on something. He came up with a mangled bicycle. There was a smashed wicker basket on the front of it. "Safe to say Shirley is dead. Warrick is a bike killer. I once knew a serial killer."

Ned put his hands on Mississippi's shoulders. "There, there. It was only a bike. It could have easily been you with how careless that young man was bein'. Shifters."

"You keep taking jabs at shifters, Ned, and I'm going to take you out back and show you where a bear goes in the woods," said Petey, putting up his dukes. "You know I can. I've done it to you before. Your hocus-pocus can't stand up against my raw manliness."

Mississippi yelped and pushed between the men.

Curt rushed forward and did the same, leaving his body pressed close to the woman's. In an instant his body was responding, leaving no room for interpretation on what he thought of her. He stiffened and hoped she didn't notice.

She brushed against the evidence and spun around to face him, her eyes wide, her mouth falling open.

Crap. She noticed.

Petey leaned around them. "Ned, I thought we could set old ways aside now that it's been so long, but it's plain to see you still think you're better than everyone else. You're still sore Marie-Claire only had eyes for me before the dark magic came into play. I bet you had a hand in what them Corduas witches did. There was talk of you being linked to it all."

Ned huffed. "I do not have to stand here and be insulted by a vagrant like you. Looks like you rolled out of a gutter. You've really let yourself go, Peter. Not that you had far to fall. You never were worth much. Looks as if you proved most of us right."

Curt rounded on the man. "Hey. Watch it. That man is like family to me. I don't care how rough around the edges he is or how much he smells like fish and whiskey half of the time, he's good people. Check that tone or I'll do it for you."

"Aww, shucks. Thanks, Warrick. Sorry I bit you," said Petey. "And sorry one of your ex-girlfriends wants you dead."

Mississippi snorted.

Curt rubbed the back of his neck. "Thanks, Petey."

Mississippi put her hand on Ned's arm. "Mr. Flanks, I'm fine. Really. Thank you for checking. Everything here will be all right. I'm sure you're very busy this morning. This is getting in the way of your day."

The man nodded. Reluctantly, Ned walked off but not without shooting dagger looks back at Petey.

Petey put his thumbs in his ears, waved his hands, stuck out his tongue, and blew raspberries at the man.

Curt sighed.

Mississippi burst into laughter. "Oh, Mémé said you were a card. She wasn't kidding. Did I hear the other man say y'all are going to Luc's? Hells Gate Inn is just up the way a bit. I can show y'all the way."

"Thank you," said Petey, putting his arm out for her.

She took it and then glanced at Curt. "If you'd be so kind as to bring Shirley and not run anyone else over, that would be great."

He blushed but smiled all the same. "Okay, but only if you let me take you to dinner."

Petey winked at her. "Warrick is an okay boy. Your grandmother will approve of him. Though he's marked for death so maybe make him prepay for dinner in case ninjas leap out and get him before it's over."

She paused. "Marked for death?"

Petey nodded. "Got a curse on him. Pretty sure one of his exes put it on him. He makes change because of it. Didn't you notice all the money around him?"

Her lip curled. "He's so rich he drops money everywhere?"

Petey shook his head and then stopped. "Well, yes, but normally his money isn't charged with dark magic and death notes."

A sheriff's car pulled to a stop next to Curt. A guy who had to be six foot seven stepped out. He looked to be around the age of forty. His black hair was cut in a messy, wavy style. His deep brown eyes were the same color as Mississippi's. His skin tone was the same as well. Curt looked between the two and realized they were more than likely related. Curt was hardly a small guy, but the newcomer was so muscular he looked like he might be able to lift Sunshine with one hand.

The man set his sights on Mississippi. "You all right, darlin'?"

"I'm okay. Shirley didn't survive. I was pushing her across the street, heading back to my shop, when Mr. Flashy ran the stop sign," said Mississippi. "Good thing I wasn't on her or I'd be mangled too."

Petey smiled. "Mr. Flashy is going to take her to dinner. She's gonna make him pay up front in the event of ninjas."

The man didn't bat an eye at Petey's

oddness. He did, however, level a hard gaze on Curt. "You ran the stop sign and nearly killed my baby girl?"

His baby girl?

The blood drained from Curt's face.

The man came at him quickly.

The next Curt knew Mississippi was in front of him. She put her arms out. "Daddy, no killing Curt."

Her father paused. "Curt Warrick?"

Wilber's laugh could be heard with ease even though he was still in the van. "Your reputation precedes you, Warrick. Hey, Walden, can you lend me a hand? Got a doomsday issue in here."

Walden peered into the van. "Wilber Messing, that you in there?"

"Yep, Peugeot, it's me. If my rock-for-brains grandson-in-law could get out of the way, that would be great. I could come out and greet you. We hunters have to stick together."

With a grunt Hugh stepped out of the van.

Curt glanced at Mississippi. Her father was a hunter? That meant she was one too.

She certainly didn't look like a lethal weapon. She looked more like hugging trees was her favorite thing to do.

Walden walked around to the side of the van and peered in at Wilber. "That a Destiny Vase?"

"It was until Warrick got near it," snapped Wilber. "Luc can help contain the power if we get it to him."

Walden lifted the radio on his hip. "Daisy, track down Louis. Tell him to meet me at the antiques shop, code red. Put a call into Hells Gate and see if Luc is in town. If so, have him meet us at the antiques shop."

"Can do, Sherriff," said a woman from the other end of the radio.

He then looked at Wilber. "You have enough control over it to move to my squad car? I'll get us to the safe room at the shop. I think I have something on hand that can contain it."

Wilber eased out of the van, pushing past Hugh before giving Curt a hard look.

Walden followed behind the hunter and paused in front of Curt. His gaze went to the flask that had apparently fallen out of the van in the commotion and was now lying on the ground near the driver's side.

"It's not what you're thinking," said Curt.

"I think there is a flask that had lemonade in it and that you're standing in the middle of cursed pirate treasure."

"Told ya it looked like pirate treasure," said Petey.

Curt glanced down at the coins and then to Petey. "It didn't have whiskey in it?"

Petey shook his head. "Promised Kelsey I'd go easier on the stuff."

With a slight shrug, Curt stared up at Walden. "Never mind. It's exactly what it looks like."

"You could have killed my baby girl," said the man sternly.

"I know. And I'm sorry. I'll replace Laverne."

"Laverne?" asked Walden.

Wilber sighed. "He means Shirley, but the boy's head is on sideways since he saw your daughter. If I'm not mistaken, your baby laid another curse on him. Not that Warrick didn't have enough as it was."

"She's a hunter," said Curt, stiffening at the words. "Her words can't curse me. That could only happen if she was a magic of some sort."

"About that," said Mississippi, her face turning pink.

Walden whipped around and looked at his daughter. "Missi?"

She closed her eyes and then nodded.

"Tell me you didn't, darlin'," said the sheriff.

She blinked up at him. "It flew out. I didn't mean it."

Petey nodded. "Same thing happened to her grandmother once. She was angry with me over a misunderstanding and she cursed me a good one. I was in Warrick's spot."

Walden stiffened. "You Captain Petey?"

Petey's chest puffed out. "Hear that, Warrick? I'm well-known here too."

Curt played everything that had been said over again in his head. His eyes widened. "Hold on, you're a hunter with magic?"

"Yes," Mississippi said, her voice barely there.

Walden let out a long breath. "Wilber, hop in my car, I'll get you and the vase to the shop. Missi, take Warrick with you to your shop. Stay close to him. If what I smell is right, he ain't got a lick of magic in him. He's some sort of cat-shifter, but a non-magic. And if he has a curse from you on him, in addition to whatever other curse he came with, he's gonna need all the magical help he can get. I'll have Daisy track down your mother, grandmother, and sister to help."

"Take him with me?" asked Mississippi, her eyes wide. "To my magic shop?"

A woman with blonde hair and yellow glasses came walking towards them. She smiled. "Oh, Mississippi, you found him! Good."

Walden inclined his head. "Ms. Cherry."

Mississippi shook her head. "No. Tell me one of the other guys is the one. Not that one. Not Mr. Flashy."

Confused, Curt simply stared between the women.

Ms. Cherry eyed him up and down

slowly as if he were a slab of meat. "Oh, sugar, he's a fine-lookin' male. Very fine. Take him down to the docks and have him take his shirt off. The ladies will love it. Gonna make some good-lookin' babies with you."

Walden spun around and had Curt shoved against the van in the flash of an eye. "Touch my baby girl or try any baby makin' and cursed coins will be the least of your worries. I'll take you out to the swamps and ain't no one gonna find your body again, boy."

Curt put his hands up slowly to signal surrender.

Jake was suddenly there, prying the man back from him. "Sheriff Peugeot, take it easy. Wilber is annoyed with Curt right now, but he'll vouch for him. Warrick is a good guy."

"That don't mean he's allowed to mate with my daughter," said the man.

Curt gasped. "Mate? What? No!"

He was going to add more about how he was not mating to anyone when his gaze flickered to Mississippi. The harder he looked at her, the more he could see himself with her for the long haul.

"Tell him that his daughter isn't your mate," stressed Jake.

Curt's entire body tightened, and he strained to get the words out that Jake wanted to hear. When it became obvious they weren't coming out of Curt's mouth, he sighed. "I can't tell him that."

Walden made a go at him again.

Hugh pushed in and helped Jake keep the man back.

Leo was out of the van now too and walking closer to Curt. "Warrick, the chaos spell is at work. Do your best not to help it along."

Mississippi came closer, looking at him like he might bite. "Tell my father you're not my mate. No way is my mate some loaded guy who sneezes gold coins while driving a hippie van."

Curt soaked in the sight of her. She had to be the sexiest woman he'd ever seen in all his life. The fact that she'd cursed him should have really turned him off. It didn't.

Strangely, it kind of turned him on. He raked his gaze over her slowly.

"Pretty sure Warrick is mentally undressing her," said Petey, which made Walden growl.

"Missi, I heard you were nearly run over by a semi," said a woman with long, dark, curly hair.

"Jasmine? A semi?" asked Mississippi. "No. Sorry, the grapevine already has it blown out of proportion. I was nearly run over by that flowered nightmare behind me."

Jasmine glanced at Curt and then gasped. "I know you. You're the out-of-towner who is trying to buy Missi's other lot! I had a vision of you!"

"He's the rich big shot who is trying to buy my land?" asked Mississippi.

Jasmine nodded and then looked as if she was about to attack him. "He sure is. My spirit guides showed him to me plain as day. That's him all right."

Mississippi bent, and the next Curt knew, the woman had a handful of cursed coins and was throwing them at him, shouting additional curses at him as she did—these curses were a little more colorful than the last. It took Ms. Cherry, Jasmine, Walden, and Jake to get her back from him.

Her father grunted. "Mississippi, stop havin' a dyin' duck fit!"

Hugh laughed. "Oh yeah. She is totally your mate. Fate would hand you a woman who can't stand you or your money. I really hope she's allergic to you or shoots rainbows out of her fingertips."

Petey moved closer. "She's much prettier than the women you normally pick, Warrick. They look like women I once knew when I was on shore leave."

Mississippi's eyes widened, and she tried to get to Curt again, threatening his man parts as she did.

He stepped back.

Walden shook his head. "Tell me we're all wrong. Tell me my baby girl's fated mate is not him."

"Hey. I'm a catch," said Curt.

Wilber snorted. "Says you. I already told you that you're making the heathen look good."

Hugh grinned and waggled his brows.

Mississippi shook her head. "No. He's not my...he can't be my...no way he's my...oh fiddlesticks. Tell me he's not my mate!"

"I'd love to, darlin'," said her father. "But my gut is screamin' at me that he is, and you cursed him. Your momma is gonna want to hear about this. Between you and me, she cursed me too when I first met her. She, like her momma, was not a fan of hunters back then. I grew on her. Just like this fool will grow on you."

Curt huffed.

Jake sighed. "Someone cursed Warrick on our way here too."

Petey nodded. "He's very cursable. Can't drive worth a darn but he's super cursable. Everyone has to be good at something. Warrick is good at getting cursed and charming the ladies. He's real good at buying up property too. He's into real estate investments. Bet if he gets your land he'll make a ton of money off it. That'll make you a rich woman, being mated to him and all."

Mississippi tried to come at Curt again and her expression didn't look friendly.

Walden caught his daughter around the waist. "Darlin', stop."

"He wants to take my property, Daddy. And he nearly killed me while actually murdering Shirley," she protested.

Curt moved towards her, pushing through the crowd of people. He touched Walden's arm lightly. "Sir, please. She's fine. You can put her down."

The man's eyes widened. "Son, I'm not sure how they do things up North where y'all are from, but down here when one of our women are this riled up, you do not set them free to finish what they started. Well, not unless you're like Deathwish Dexter or Apocalypse Arnold."

Petey slapped his upper thigh and then looked at the men around him. "Told you I knew them and that they were real!"

Chapter Nine

MISSI STOPPED STRUGGLING against her father's hold. He released her but remained close, knowing her well. She glanced at Curt. As angry as she was with him for breaking Shirley and for being the big shot who was trying to acquire her property, it was hard to deny the fact the man was incredibly good looking.

As if reading Missi's mind, Ms. Cherry grinned and winked. "Congrats! I'm so happy for you two. I'm gonna have to help your momma and grandmother plan a weddin' celebration. It will be so much fun. We haven't had one since your momma and daddy got hitched. That celebration didn't go over as planned. I had to try to keep your grandmother from hexin' your daddy."

Missi groaned. "I already told you that I'm not dating anyone. There is no wedding. No celebration is needed. But anyone who wants to can hex him. Apparently, he's very curseable."

Ms. Cherry looked between them. "But you will be married very soon. Come on, everyone. This nice young man is gonna take Missi and what's left of Shirley back to her shop. Hopefully, he'll be able to sweet talk his way into her good graces."

A large man with dark brown hair clamped his hands down on Curt's shoulders and rubbed them. "If you could refrain from having your mate curse you more than she already has, that would be great. Like Petey said, you're already making change. I'd hate to see what else you start doing."

"Hugh?" asked Curt, looking a bit green around the edges. Apparently, he was as on board with the idea they were something more to each other as Missi was.

That should have given her comfort.

Oddly, it didn't.

Hugh smiled. "I was in your position not that long ago, Curt. Don't fight it. Just let Fate do with you what it may. Resistance is futile. You'll be happy in the end. You may or may not have to curse using baked goods, but whatever."

Curt faced her fully before looking to where Shirley lay, bent beyond repair. Missi had loved the bike since she'd first gotten her when she was fourteen. It had once been her grandmother's.

Curt went to the mangled bicycle and lifted it with one hand. He then reached up with his other and began to bend Shirley back into something that marginally resembled her original shape. She had a long way to go before she'd be fixed, if she even could be. Seeing Curt bend metal with no effort reminded her of what Mr. Flanks had said. Curt was a shifter. They tended to be very strong. Some types of supernaturals were. Others had the same strength as a human —such was the case with Missi.

Curt tried to bend Shirley back into shape more and her smashed basket broke off and fell to the street. "I'll buy you a new one."

Jasmine snorted. "That will never work to get her to calm down. That bike was special to her. You can't just ride in here in the Peace Mobile and think you can buy anything you want. She's not for sale. And while I'm at it, I like the van. Not you."

Petey rubbed the van's side. "Hear that, Sunshine? She likes you. I told you that you're cherry. Don't listen to what Hugh and Curt say about you. You're a beautiful peace wagon."

"What a shocker," said Jasmine, eyeing Curt as if she might go for the jugular. It's what best friends did for one another. "He doesn't even like the van."

Missi nudged her friend lightly and shook her head, wanting Jasmine to stop. "Jas."

They shared a look and Jasmine nodded, looking less than pleased.

Missi offered a warm smile. "Can you come back to the shop with Curt and me? I'm going to need your help with a spell to counter what I did to him."

"What did you do to him?" asked Jasmine.

Missi tugged at her lower lip. "I might have sort of cursed him when I was in a fit of anger."

Jasmine's eyes widened a second before she burst into laughter.

Curt bemoaned, "It's not that funny."

"No. It is that funny," said Hugh. "Unless you end up dead, then it runs out of funny fast. No one but me gets to kill my best buddy."

Curt grinned at his friend. "Thanks, man. That means a lot to me."

Petey looked between the men. "Do I sense a hug coming on? I'm in!"

Missi's father rubbed his temple. "Darlin', didn't Mémé Marie-Claire have a long talk with you about mindin' what you say when you're upset?"

She had. And Missi had never had an issue with it in the past. It was just a precautionary thing her grandmother told each of her grandchildren. Or it had been.

Missi closed her eyes a moment, ashamed of her lack of control on her magic. She was better than that. She was the one who normally schooled others on magic's proper use and the need to exercise extreme caution when wielding it. There was only one silver lining she could find to the ordeal. "In my defense, he already came cursed."

"Fair point," said Curt, coming to her aid while he propped Shirley against the van with great care, as if she could possibly be damaged more. He then eased closer to Missi and the coins on the street. He reached into his pockets and pulled out more, letting them fall to the ground as well. "As my friends keep pointing out, I'm making change. I'm like a walking quarter machine, if the machine spit out cursed gold pieces with weird symbols on them."

Weird symbols? In her stretch of irritation, she'd not stopped to notice any markings on the coins. She'd pretty much just seen them as something to throw at Curt. Not one of her finest moments by any means. It was also one her brothers wouldn't let her live down when they caught wind of it. York would claim she was just like him. Louis would tell her she was unrefined. She was kind of surprised they weren't already there.

News traveled fast in a small town.

Missi glanced down at the coins on the ground, taking a moment to actually look at them as more than objects to be thrown. On one side was the head of a lion. On the other was a symbol she'd seen before. "What are you doing with Blackbeard's treasure?"

"Blackbeard?" asked Curt. "Like the pirate?"

Petey nodded so hard his knit cap needed adjusted. "You never believe me. I swear you people think all I do is make stuff up. I don't. It's all true."

Curt's head whipped around as he stared at Petey. "He's real?"

Petey rolled his eyes. "Of course he is, Warrick. Why would anyone make up knowing a pirate? This is like the time you all thought I was making up seeing a walking squid wearing a wristwatch. I wasn't. That turned out to be Sigmund."

"Blackbeard got put in a bottle once,"

said Missi's father. "One of my sons' more noteworthy stunts."

"Shiver Me Timbers isn't open yet today. Or at least it wasn't not that long ago," said Missi to her father.

Her father lifted a brow. "Hmm. Strange. He's normally open today. There wasn't a notice on the town bulletin board about him bein' closed extra this week. Anyone talk to him lately? I haven't seen him in a few days but that's not out of the ordinary."

"I haven't seen him in a few days either," said Missi.

"That marking is from Blackbeard's treasure. But I don't remember seeing lions on any of the gold pieces he showed us," said Jasmine as she pushed in close to Missi. "My spirit guides are telling me it's all as it should be but I'm not buying it."

"Spirit guides?" asked Curt, looking around.

The women knelt, each reaching for a coin at the same time. A tall man in an army jacket bent quickly and touched

Jasmine's wrist, preventing her from making contact with any coins.

"They burned me. I think they might have something on them that prevents other magics from interfering," he said, his gaze lingering on Jasmine longer than need be.

Was that a spark of interest she saw between the two of them?

"Missi touched the coins already when she was throwing them at the cursed guy." Jasmine didn't make contact with them. "Did they burn you then, Missi?"

"No. They didn't," she replied. "They felt cold to me."

Army jacket guy touched one and jerked his hand back fast, blowing on his fingers. "Ouch!"

Jasmine swallowed hard and moved her hand back and forth over the coins on the ground. "I sense the spell now. It's cloaked. Wow. That is powerful magic on those. More than one kind of magic too. It feels like three or four. How can that be?"

Missi's stomach tightened as she thought of the implications. Someone actually wanted Curt dead. Looking up, she locked gazes with him. "Who else have you tried to run over or am I the only lucky lady?"

His full lips quirked before a sexy smile slid over his handsome face. "Just you."

"Thanks. I think." She remained bent, but he joined them all.

The four of them stayed crouched around the coins.

Jasmine kept moving her hand over the gold pieces, careful not to touch them. "When did you first notice them appearing?"

"Few hours back," said the guy in the army jacket.

"You're familiar to me, boy," said Missi's father to the man. "Where have I seen you before?"

Wilber, who was now sitting in the front passenger side of the sheriff's car, leaned out, still holding a vase on his lap. For a second it seemed to glow with white light. "He's a Gibbons, Walden."

Shock covered her father's face. "No. How? I thought that line of hunters died out."

Wilber nodded to Jake, who Missi knew because he'd been friends with her family since before she was born. Jake had spent time in Hedgewitch Cove before heading off to the big city to be a police detective. He'd later moved to Maine for a change of pace. "The centaur saved one of their lives way back when. His own kind turned on him for it."

Her father shook his head, his gaze going to Jake. "That's why your people cast you out?"

Jake inclined his head but said nothing on the matter.

"All these years and I never knew," said her father softly. "You know you always have a place here should you want it. Maybe we'll get lucky and mate you off at some point."

Jake grinned. "I'm mated now."

"What?" asked her father. "When did this happen and who is the lucky young woman?"

Army jacket guy groaned. "My sister. I'd argue that she's the cursed one in this scenario. She got him."

MANDY M. ROTH

Missi's father laughed. "Jake, your mate is from a line of hunters with magic powers?"

Jake nodded. "She is. Her name is Kelsey and she's so incredibly perfect, Walden. I don't know how I made it through the day without her in my life before. You once told me that was how you felt when you and Murielle ended up mated. I never understood it then. I get it now. We've a little one on the way. I wanted to be back home with her, but she pretty much threw me into the van to hit the road with this group."

Missi's father laughed more. "Ah, pregnancy hormones. I remember them well. Murielle done tossed me out on my ear for a week with each pregnancy. Actually, two weeks with the twins. Pretty sure a week for each baby she was carryin'. I slept in the RV parked out in the driveway. If her mother would have gotten her way, I'd have slept with the fishes, if you know what I mean."

Missi had never heard that story. She did know that her father and her grandmother did not see eye to eye. With the long history of hunters killing witches, the last person on earth Mémé had wanted one of her children mated to was a hunter. It didn't matter that her father's line of hunters had been cursed long ago to have supernatural blood in them. He was still a hunter. And while her parents had been mated for a century, that didn't mean Mémé had taken a shine to her father. And her father certainly hadn't grown any fonder of Mémé.

Jake snorted. "Oh, I'm positive Marie-Claire would have preferred that. I'm shocked she hasn't tried."

Missi's father flashed a cocksure smile. "Who says she hasn't?"

"Daddy?" asked Missi. "Ms. Cherry was joking about the hexing thing at your wedding celebration, right?"

He winked at her. "It's fine, darlin'. And it's between me and Mémé. We've played the game too long to stop now."

"Want a cookie?" asked Petey out of nowhere. "You could give her some too. Trust me, it will help."

Hugh, Curt, and Leo shouted "no" at the same time.

Missi and Jasmine glanced at one another and shrugged. Men were very odd creatures.

She began gathering up the gold coins in her hands. Strong, large male hands moved over hers with a speed that stunned her. Heat flared through her palms at the man's touch. With a sharp intake of breath, she realized it was Curt who was touching her.

"I know you said they don't burn you like they do Leo, but what if whatever chaos-death-thing that is on them gets on you? I don't want you hurt," he said, his deep voice softening slightly. "I'll happily keep on making change and carrying around a death note so long as it means you're not affected too."

She simply stared at him, his words moving her. Her eyes misted up and she swallowed hard in an attempt to keep from being outright emotional. It didn't exactly work. She sniffled.

Petey was behind her quickly. He

whipped out a rather used-looking handkerchief and thrust it at her, sniffling himself. "No one cries alone on my watch."

Curt snorted.

Missi stared at the handkerchief as if it might bite. "Thank you, but I'm good."

He blew his nose on it and then shoved it back into his pocket.

Curt tipped his head and lowered his voice. "Sorry about him."

"He's fine," she said, continuing to hold the cursed coins, too swept up in his green gaze to think much beyond it. Why did the man have to be so good-looking? What was it with rich men? Did a secret factory spit them out? You-Know-Who had been very attractive as well. Jasmine had always said his smile was too white. That anyone with a smile that white should not be trusted.

Jasmine had been correct.

Curt's brow creased. "Did you hear me, Mississippi?"

She blinked up at Curt and realized he'd been speaking to her. "Huh?"

Jasmine groaned. "Not again. Didn't You-Know-Who teach you anything?"

"What?" asked Curt. "Who knows who?"

Petey grunted. "No, Warrick. Know-You-Who. Not Who-Knows-Who."

Missi couldn't help but laugh at the absurdity of it all. Her laugh came out more like a strangled cry.

"Mississippi?" asked Curt. "Are you okay?"

"She goes by Missi," said Jasmine to Curt, her tone clipped. Missi knew her best friend was only looking out for her and she appreciated it, but it wasn't needed. "And if you dare break her heart I'll send a horde of zombies after you and they'll tear you limb from limb before they feed you to the gators."

"I'll kick his butt for the fun of it for you," said the man in the army jacket to Jasmine.

"Leo," snapped Curt.

Leo grinned. "What? She's prettier than you."

"Can we not unleash a zombie horde on anyone?" asked Missi. "Save that for after I go to dinner with him."

"So, it's a yes to dinner?" asked Curt, sounding hopeful.

Missi blew out a long breath. "I didn't mean that. I just meant…um…yes. It's a yes so long as you don't think of driving in town again."

"Deal," he said quickly.

Petey bent over them. "She's a step up from Hugh holding you, huh? I don't know what Penelope sees in him. He's not that good-looking."

Curt grinned.

Hugh rolled his eyes.

Petey kept going. "I'm actually ordained by more than one church and religion. I can totally marry the two of you if you want. With all the matings happening in Everlasting I went on the internet and got certified in as many things as I could. Seemed wise and handy." He then put the back of his hand to the side of his mouth. "Warrick, her father looks like he could break you in two without really trying so I'd advise keeping a chaperone around until you mate her proper. Want for me to do it now? By the power vested in me, I now pronounce you Lion and Witch. You may kiss the witch. There. It's a done deal."

Ms. Cherry smiled wide. "Oh, that was lovely."

Petey nodded. "Thank you."

Missi jerked her hands out of Curt's and the coins fell away. As they hit the ground, they vanished. Every single one of them disappeared into thin air like they'd never been there at all.

A round of gasps followed.

Missi touched the ground, half expecting her hand to go through it. That didn't happen.

Jasmine stood slowly, and Leo assisted her, holding her arm gently. "Do you feel the residual power in the air?"

"Yes," replied Leo.

"Not to break up the moment, but this doomsday vase is less than pleased," said Wilber. "I've got some other artifacts I need stored safely. They're in the crate in the van. The one Warrick kicked and broke. I'm starting to think Warrick was cursed from the very start of this trip."

Missi couldn't think much past the fact

that Curt's face was close to hers. She had a ton of things she wanted to say, not to mention more yelling she wanted to do over his murder of Shirley, but none of that came out.

He leaned, and his lips drew even closer to hers. His eyes closed and just before his lips would have met hers, Petey lost his footing and fell right onto Curt, knocking him backwards, away from Missi, and onto his backside on the street next to Shirley. The bike then bumped Missi, knocking her down as well.

Petey landed in Curt's lap with a loud oomph.

Jake snorted. "Is it me or was Warrick about to kiss Missi only to get a Petey instead?"

"It wasn't you," said Wilber.

Jake's eyes widened. "Curt, you really are cursed."

"Tell me about it," said Curt with a groan as he tried but failed to get Petey off his lap. "Hugh, a little help would be nice."

Petey looked at Curt, still on his lap. "I don't know. You're married now. Wait. That is a curse. Jumping jack-o-lanterns, you are so cursed, Warrick. Best of luck to you. Married life has neutered every male I know."

Hugh, who was laughing so hard he wasn't making any sound, bent and lifted Petey off Curt with ease. Curt then pushed to his feet rather ungracefully and extended a hand to Missi.

She eyed it like it might bite. "I don't know. If I touch you again, will a plane fall out of the sky on us?"

"I already had a Petey fall on me so I'm ready for anything," he said with a wink. "Wife, can I help you up?"

She tensed at the word *wife*. "Only if you don't joke about that again."

"Who is joking?" asked Petey. "It's official. I married ya both. You were there. You should know this already."

Curt grinned at the older man. "Funny."

Petey shrugged, looking lost as to what was amusing.

Ms. Cherry blinked and touched her

collarbone. "I, for one, thought it was simply lovely. We'll need to celebrate."

"Sounds good to me. Might want to wait until Warrick isn't so cursed," replied Petey.

She put her hand in Curt's and he eased her upright. Stepping back would have been a really smart move especially considering the day she'd had so far and Ms. Cherry's words of warning on falling in love, but that wasn't what happened. Missi eased closer to the man and found her gaze locking on his neck, where his expensive collared shirt was open. He smelled like expensive cologne. It was amazing.

She sighed.

Jasmine leaned in close to her. "Way to stand your ground there, Missi. No rich bigwig is going to run over you."

"Hey, is it me or is there a guy in a tracksuit waving his arms at us frantically down the street there, all while missing a head?" asked Leo. "I'm seeing that right, aren't I?"

Petey jumped up and down, pointing in the direction of Headless Hank, who was down the street in front the bookstore. "See! I told you I knew a guy who lost his head. That's Hank. He's the barber. Gives great haircuts but try to catch him on Wednesdays. That's the day his head stays home from work. He's a talker when his head is on the counter at work. Best to just get the body or you're there for hours."

Missi's father nodded. "That's true. Hank is a talker. You get him goin' and there is no stoppin' him."

Curt's lips twitched. "This place has a headless guy?"

Hugh stepped back. "This might be the strangest town ever."

"Thank you," said Missi, Ms. Cherry, and Jasmine at the same time.

Ms. Cherry gave a slight wave. "I'm off to find Marie-Claire to give her the good news. I looked for her before at the cemetery, but she wasn't there. I'm sure I'll find her soon enough."

With that she hurried away.

"Hedgewitch Cove has their own version of the headless horseman," said Leo, looking surprised.

Missi moved even closer to Curt, feeling drawn to him. "What do you mean *our* version? He's the *only* version. Hank *is* the headless horseman. I mean, he was. He stopped riding around on a horse way before I was born. He drives a car now. I wish he'd go back to the horse; it was better for the environment."

Curt's hand found hers. "How does a headless guy drive a car?"

"How does a guy with a head not know how to drive a van?" she countered.

He grinned.

She sighed again.

Jasmine groaned.

"Is that a boxer dog running down the street at us with a head in its mouth?" asked Hugh.

Missi tensed. "Oh no. Furfur has Hank's head."

"Again?" asked her father. "Damn hellhound. Luc really has gotta get better invisible fencin'. Maybe sprinkle holy water around the property or somethin'. Anything to keep that mutt from wanderin' around town."

Jasmine swatted Leo in the gut lightly. "Hurry. Go to that side to block him. The rest of you fan out."

Just then Sigmund appeared behind Furfur, running full force at the dog. He whistled, and Furfur came to a complete stop, sitting like a good boy in the center of Water Street. He dropped Hank's head.

"I really thought a head from a headless guy would be bloody and gory," said Hugh.

"Me too," added Leo.

"Nah," said Jasmine. "Magic took his head. Magic keeps it pristine. Also helps him be able to function without it on his shoulders."

The rest of Hank rushed out into the street and swooped up the head. He pointed at the dog with his head tucked under his arm. "Bad dog!"

Missi failed to keep from laughing at the sight.

Sigmund looked down the street at them and then smiled wide.

Petey put out his arms. "Bails, I missed ya! Let's hug. Don't hug Warrick. He's cursed so many times I lost count!"

Chapter Ten

"STILL NOTHING?" asked Missi of her father who was on the other end of the phone.

"No, darlin'," he said. "Louis showed up about an hour ago and has been helpin' Wilber, Leo, Jasmine, and I sort through texts down here in the basement of the antique shop. We can't find anythin' on the curse Curt has over him."

Since her brother's shop sat on a goldmine of information that was in an underground bunker that extended well out and under the property his shop sat on, something should have been found. Hunter libraries and artifact-holding facilities were always stocked with information on just about any supernatural or curse out there. The very fact nothing was turning up was alarming in itself.

"What do you want me to do with him?" she asked, glancing across her shop at Curt, who was sitting on the stool behind the counter, flipping through a magic book on spells. So far, their day together had consisted of her mother showing up at the shop with Jasmine to help ward it with protection spells since everyone's main concern was the death note end of the curses.

Oddly, Curt hadn't seemed altogether that bothered with it all, and she had to wonder how often he had people wanting him dead or if it was just the way he handled difficult matters.

It didn't look like their dinner date was going to happen. Not unless they figured out who had cursed Curt to start with, why they wanted him dead, and what Blackbeard's treasure had to do with it all. Basically, it was all still a mystery and they were no closer to answers than they had been in the middle of the street, hours ago.

"Has anyone seen Blackbeard yet?" asked Missi, drawing Curt's attention.

Her father was silent a moment. "No. Not yet."

"Nothing?" asked Missi. "And you're sure York didn't do anything stupid again?"

"Darlin', we've not been able to reach York or any of his crew members."

Missi tensed. "He should have been back hours ago."

"I'm sure he's fine. That boy knows the water like no one else. He's an expert boater and fisherman. That being said, Petey, Sig, Hugh, and Jake took out a boat. They're headin' to the area York was supposed to be in today. They should be reportin' in soon."

"Is Mom back with you?" she asked, worried for her family. "Has anyone checked on Mémé?"

"Darlin', calm down. Your momma is with your grandmother and sister as we speak. I've got your cousins lookin' for Blackbeard. Ms. Cherry, Flanks, and Hank all know what's goin' on so that means the entire town is now aware. Everyone is on the lookout for him."

"Ms. Cherry told me there was a loud ruckus a few nights back, not far from here. She thinks she heard Mr. Flanks and Blackbeard shouting, followed by a big boom," said Missi, unsure why she felt the need to tell her father.

"Odd, she didn't mention it to me when I asked her if she knew anythin'. She did say she was at your shop this morning though stockin' up on supplies."

Missi nodded. "She was. She bought everything she needed to banish Rockey from the theater again."

Her father sighed. "Or to banish any spirit from anywhere?"

Missi hadn't thought of it that way. "I guess. Yes. But what would she have to gain by banishing Blackbeard?"

"What did any of her relatives have to gain by castin' out nearly a hundred residents from Hedgewitch Cove? Petey was one of them. Flanks's people helped with that ordeal. Your grandmother still holds a grudge with him over that," said her father.

"Did Ms. Cherry say anything else about Flanks and Blackbeard?"

"No, but I did see Flanks outside of the shaved iced stand this morning on my way to the restaurant. He was acting different. I don't know. I'm sure it was nothing. He's not what you're making him out to be. He's pretty harmless."

"Mississippi, when you look at your grandmother and mother, do you see dangerous women?" he asked.

"Of course not."

"Yet, they're two of the most powerful women in the state. The damage they could do if they ever set their mind to it would be somethin' all right," he stated. "What I'm sayin' is, don't go judgin' a book by its cover. Just because somethin' looks sweet and innocent doesn't mean it can't be dangerous."

"Momma would not be happy to hear you say that about her or Mémé."

Her father chuckled. "Darlin', she's the one who told me that very thing. It's somethin' her mother had impressed upon her all her life. I have a feelin' it dates back to what happened between your grandmother and Petey. I don't think your grandmother has ever forgiven herself for cursing Petey the way she did. I'm told before it happened that he was a different man. That he had his act together."

Missi cringed. "I'm just like her. I cursed Curt."

"Yes, but thankfully, your witch side is diluted somewhat by the hunter side," he said softly. "That means your curse probably won't cause the same havoc the one on Petey has."

She exhaled slowly. "I wish I could take it back. Curt didn't deserve my angry words. Mémé warned me. She told me to always mind what I say when angry."

"Darlin', all will be well. Right now, I need you to sit tight with that cursed mate of yours," her father said, his voice even. "But tell him he's not allowed to touch you. Ever."

Missi glanced nervously at Curt and then focused on the sage rack. "I'm sure he's not my you-know-what. Can we discuss this later?"

Her father snorted. "Darlin', he's a cat-shifter. He's heard this entire conversation even if you're up in your apartment and he's down in the shop. His hearin' is that good. And as much as I'm not ready for any of my girls to get married, especially not my baby, your mother called the minute she left your place informin' me Curt is most certainly your mate. But I stand by my no touchin' you rule. He can just admire you from afar until you're like eighty or something. You're immortal. So is he. It will be fine."

Gulping, Missi turned slightly to find Curt sitting on the stool, holding the spell book, grinning up at her. He winked.

Without thought, she grabbed a ritual candle and threw it at him.

He deflected it with the spell book and laughed.

She groaned. "Daddy, I cannot stay locked in here with him. I might kill him myself. The curses won't have to bother."

"That a girl," said her father. "Want me to send your cousins over? When they heard you've a mate and that he's in town, the first thing they wanted to do was rough him up. Louis wanted to interview him to see if he was suitable for you. You know Louis."

She smiled. "Did he explain where he was?"

"Said he was a parish over when his car broke down for no good reason. You know, hearin' him tell me about his mornin' and listenin' to your sister tell me about her ordeal tryin' to get home travelin', added in with you nearly being run down by your mate, I'm startin' to worry all my kids are cursed."

Missi tensed. "Daddy, York."

"Is fine. I'm sure. I'm gonna reach out to Georgia and Arizona and check in on them. Somethin' is off," he said. "I love you, darlin'. Don't kill your mate. No sense dirtyin' your hands with that when a curse might do it for you."

She grunted and hung up before looking at Curt again.

"Want me to pretend I didn't hear your father confirm who we are to each other?" asked Curt, setting the spell book on the counter.

Missi leveled a hard look on him.

His eyes widened. "You have an eyebrow that arches up when you're mad at me. I'm starting to like the look."

She gave it to him more.

He cleared his throat and wiggled on the stool.

The next Missi knew, Curt was flat on his back on the floor behind the counter. She rushed to him and bent. "Are you okay?"

"My suaveness just took a nose dive, but I'm fine," he said, lying there, looking up at her.

"You're suave? Really?" she teased. "I hadn't noticed."

He reached up and touched her cheek. "So I like to think."

She nodded. "I can see that. You seem to think very highly of yourself. Sig wasn't wrong about you."

He brushed her hair back from her face and she found herself bending over him more. "Well, I am a stud. What can I say?"

She giggled.

"So, about the no-touching-you rule,"

he said, his voice deep. "Think we might be able to make an exception since I'm marked for death and all? Like a final meal?"

"Who do you think cursed you?" she asked.

"You mean, besides you?" He grinned in a sexy manner.

She remained in place. "Yes. Besides me. I heard Petey mention an ex-girlfriend cursing you. Is that what happened?"

"Honestly, I have no clue. It's a total mystery to me. It's been a while since I dated anyone. Well, not that you can call what I do dating," he said before seeming to think better of it.

"And what is it you do, if it's not dating?" she inquired, already knowing the answer. It didn't exactly sit well with her, but she wasn't sure. The man couldn't possibly be her mate. What he did and didn't do should not have mattered to her in the least.

But it did.

One moment they were staring into each other's eyes and the next they were kissing. Curt ran his hands into her hair and took the kiss to another level. Something near them crackled and for a moment the area seemed to fill with static electricity. It took her a moment to realize it was magic. But it wasn't her magic.

He jerked her to him harder and kissed his way to her ear, purring softly as he did. She thought about having her way with him, but now wasn't the time. Besides, he couldn't stay in Hedgewitch Cove. His life was in Everlasting.

His lips found hers once more and the kiss made her toes curl.

Missi tensed and touched his chest, breaking the kiss. "We need to get you uncursed and back to Everlasting before someone drops a house on you."

He didn't budge. He grinned. "You're not getting rid of me that easily. I'm not a Lollipop Guild member."

"What on earth are you talking about?" she asked.

He shrugged. "I'm not sure. Unlike Hugh, I've not been forced to sit through *The Wizard of Oz* movie."

She beamed. "Oh, I love that movie."

He groaned.

She stayed bent over him, her long hair hanging down like a curtain around their faces. "Did you really come down here with the intention to exploit some weird loophole about my backlot?"

He tensed and then sighed. "Yes."

She wanted to be mad at him but found it harder than it should be. "What did you want to do with it?"

He bit his lower lip. "I'd rather not say. Besides, I'm not going to do it now. Obviously."

Her brow arched up once more.

He grimaced under the weight of her stare. "Fine. I was thinking of making a fast food restaurant there or something else. I wasn't sure, but I did want to develop it."

She gasped and stood quickly, storming away from him. "Fast food!"

Curt was up and off the floor in record time, rushing behind her as she stormed towards the back of the shop. "Mississippi, wait. Hear me out. I said I'm not doing it now."

She pivoted in the pet section and looked him up and down. "You and I are very different. I'm granola and Shirley and you're, you're…fast food and fast talking! I fell for good looks and money before. I ended up hurt. I'd tell you to take your money and go but your money is currently in the form of cursed coins and lightning is likely to hit you on the way out of the door. I really hope it hits you where the goddess split you."

Curt caught her hips and boldly drew her against his powerful frame. "Hold on. Is Who-Knows-Who the good-looking loaded guy? Point me in his direction. He and I are going to discuss a few things, like the fact you're mine!"

Laughter bubbled up and through Missi's anger.

"What?" asked Curt, looking dumbfounded.

"We refer to him as You-Know-Who. Not Who-Knows-Who." She laughed more. "And you don't need to hunt him down. He's not here. He went back to his big city life. I didn't want to leave Hedgewitch Cove and I guess I wasn't a big enough draw to make him stay."

Curt stared down at her. "He wasn't your mate. I am."

"And that means what exactly? That I'm supposed to give up my friends, family, and shop and move to Maine?" she demanded.

He stayed calm. "Let's get a few things clear. I have not, nor will I ever expect you to leave your family. My friends are my family. Yes, they're very important to me and yes, I have a number of businesses in Maine, but Louisiana has something Maine doesn't."

Missi stared at him puzzled.

He grinned. "It has you. Plus, I heard there is this amazing property in town that because of a loophole in zoning might be up for grabs. How can I start my fast food empire anywhere else but here?"

"Funny." She grunted and pushed lightly on him. As she did, a gold coin fell out of thin air between them, landing on the floor. Missi was the first one to get to it. Against Curt's protests, she touched it, lifting it and standing to look at it. This one was slightly different from the others. It had the lion on one side but on the other it had a mark she knew very well.

It was the mark of the Caillat witches.

She gasped.

Curt put his hand over hers. "Missi?"

She stared up into his green eyes and the next thing she knew, she was going for his mouth again, worried for him yet wanting to be closer to him.

Curt didn't protest in the least.

He did growl into her mouth and ease her towards the floor of the shop. She glanced to the side as he kissed her neck and laughed softly as she found herself face-to-face with the cat toy section.

Why not?

Chapter Eleven

CURT FOLLOWED his mate around her small, yet cozy apartment above the magic shop. She'd spent the last forty-five minutes mumbling under her breath at him. He could only hope she wasn't cursing him—again. Even if she was, he didn't care. She was his forever and always.

It was slightly surreal, knowing he was now someone's husband. That he'd done what he'd sworn he never would—mate. He'd thought he'd wanted to be a bachelor for life. And he'd foolishly thought he knew what type of woman he wanted.

He'd been so very wrong.

It was a darn good thing Mother Nature

had kicked in with Missi, because Curt would have found a way to muck it up if left to his own devices.

He watched her as she continued muttering softly, looking annoyed with him. She wasn't exactly thrilled he'd given into his baser instincts and claimed her. He was happy he did, and he wouldn't take it back.

He snorted.

If Hugh could see him now. He'd never believe Curt did it—that he claimed someone. But Curt got it now. Got why both Hugh and Jake had been so reluctant to leave their wives back in Everlasting. Curt had been mated a fraction of the time they had, and he didn't like Missi walking ten feet from him. Being over a thousand miles away from her would kill him.

She shot him a hard look.

He failed to hide his laughter. "I said I was sorry."

"You say that a lot," she snapped. "You said it about nearly running me over, killing Shirley, and then this!"

He caught her hand in his and drew her to him. He inhaled her scent, liking the fact that she now smelled like him. His inner lion was smug with satisfaction, knowing the woman was now and would forever be his. "It just happened."

That wasn't exactly true. Had he actually tried to stop it, he might have been successful, but he hadn't tried. He'd wanted her, and he'd gotten her.

She gave him a droll look. "You just happened to bite me during, um, *that*?"

He snorted at her reluctance to actually label what they'd shared together. They were consenting adults, but apparently, they weren't allowed to use the words for it all. "Um, that? Is that how we're going to refer to—"

She stepped on his toe. "Don't say it. We aren't going to talk about it out loud."

He chuckled at her antics. "Fine but we are still going to do more of *um, that*, right?"

She blushed, and he stole a kiss. It was too hard to resist.

Being with her (more than once) in the pet toy section of the magic shop had been the best experience of his life. And he'd meant what he'd said. He hadn't intended to claim her. It just sort of happened during the height of passion. He couldn't take it back and he didn't want to. She was his wife now. There was no turning back.

And currently, his wife was giving him the evil eyebrow again.

He swallowed hard. "I'm guessing neither of us started our day thinking we'd be mated by the end of it."

She calmed slightly. "No. We didn't. Are you upset about it?"

"Upset that I have the hottest wife in the world?" he asked, dipping his head and kissing her neck.

She giggled and pushed on his chest. "Curt, no more of that. We have to be serious here. We barely know each other, and we're now considered husband and wife after what happened down in the shop."

"I'm pretty sure Petey married us on the street corner before we even got to the shop," he said with a small smile, hoping to lighten the mood. He knew she was worried about her brother. "So, we've been married longer than we thought."

She took a deep breath. "I always imagined my wedding day would be out in a grove with all my family around, celebrating. Never thought it would be next to a hippie van on a street, surrounded by cursed coins, or in the familiar toy section of my shop."

"Hon," he said softly. "We can say vows the normal way with our friends and family around us as soon as we know all of your family and friends are safe, sound, and accounted for. Besides, I heard your father mention some cousins who want to have a few words with me about being your mate. Wait until they figure out I claimed you."

Her eyes widened. "Curt, not funny. They're my dad's deputy sheriffs and each of them are a mix of hunter and shifter."

"I'm no slouch," he said, wanting to kiss her again. "Don't let my *flashiness* fool you."

She snorted.

He stole another kiss.

"Our first concern is getting you uncursed. And then it will be introducing you to my male family members. Sorry up front." She kissed his lips chastely and he nearly begged for more but resisted. "You're not very worried about being marked for death?"

He shrugged. "I was born in Everlasting. Weird is what that place does. Though Hedgewitch Cove has it beat by a longshot. We don't have a headless guy or a guy who held his gas in and then burst. We did have people-eating evil witches. That was different."

She chuckled. "Hold on. Are you serious? People-eating witches?"

"They pretty much wore their victim's skin after eating them. Babcock, party of five. They also turned into blue goo when run over by a tow truck and hit with rainbow magic."

Her eyes widened. "See, now you're going to have to take me to Everlasting, so I can see the People-Eating-Witch-Place."

He grinned and cupped her face. He'd show her the world if she let him. "Hon, say the word and I'll take you wherever you want to go. If here is where you want to be, here is where we'll stay. But can we maybe consider getting a bigger place?"

He wasn't a small guy and her apartment felt very tiny to him.

Her lips twitched, and she nodded. "Yes. I hear there is a great-sized lot behind this place that could maybe have a house built on it. Only if some big shot doesn't exploit a commercial property loophole and so long as he doesn't hurt my garden."

Curt went eerily still, afraid to move and ruin the moment. "For real? You're agreeing to letting me build you a big house? Does this mean you're done being mad at me for claiming you?"

She nodded. "I'm still mad about Shirley, but I have a lifetime to complain about that."

He swept her up in his arms and shouted with joy before walking her in the direction of the bedroom. He grinned.

"What are you doing?" she asked as she laughed and kicked her feet playfully.

"Taking you in for some of *um that*," he replied.

The next thing he knew, a tall, built man wearing nothing but a towel was there, standing in the center of the room, in his path to the bedroom.

Missi scrambled out of Curt's arms and gasped. "Blackbeard?"

That was Blackbeard?

The guy looked nothing like the portraits and drawings Curt had seen of the man in books. No. The guy looked like he was about to pose for the cover of a romance novel about falling for a pirate or something. The guy had long black hair that hung past his broad shoulders. He had a black beard that was close clipped to his jawline and silver earrings that lined both his ears. Various tattoos covered his chest and upper arms. Basically, he was the bad boy Curt heard women say they always wanted and he was standing in his mate's living room basically naked. "I changed my mind. We're so moving you to Everlasting if you have dead pirates who look like that appearing at random in your house, naked."

The man eyed him. "Who are you?"

Missi put her hand on Blackbeard's

chest and Curt saw red. "Stop touching him!"

The outburst earned him the eyebrow-glare again.

"Please?" he asked, thankful his friends weren't there to witness how he'd been neutered as well.

She groaned. "Blackbeard, meet Curt Warrick, my mate. Curt, meet Blackbeard, the pirate."

Blackbeard tipped his head. "Mate? Seriously? Fate gave you a flashy guy?"

"Why does everyone think I'm flashy?" demanded Curt.

Missi and Blackbeard shared a look.

Blackbeard eyed him and then looked at Missi. "Warrick? Isn't that Sigmund's friend's name? The one with too much money and time on his hands?"

Curt's jaw set. "The one who is mated to the woman you're currently naked and near." He moved in quickly, pushing between Missi and the pirate. He then faced Blackbeard and found himself posturing, his lion on edge.

Missi tugged on Curt's arm. "Stop it. You're being ridiculous."

He glanced over his shoulder at her. "He popped in out of thin air, wearing only a towel, and I'm the one who is being ridiculous?"

She nodded. "Yes. And he's never shown up in my apartment at all before let alone wearing nothing but a towel. I'm guessing he's here for a good reason. Not to —" She blushed more.

"If he even thinks of *um, that-ing* with you, I'll show him just how alpha I can be," warned Curt.

Missi groaned. "Stop it. We've never done that. I have admired his chest from afar but I never, okay, shutting up now."

Blackbeard laughed. "Does *um that* mean what I think it means here?"

"Yes," stated Curt with a grunt.

"Stand down there, Warrick," said Blackbeard. "I'm not here for that. I've known Mississippi since she was in her mother's belly. She's like family to me."

Curt grinned, pleased with the response until he noticed his wife frowning. He did a double take. "Hey. Try not to look so glum that he doesn't see you in that light. You're a married woman."

The eyebrow-glare returned. "Excuse me?"

Curt hadn't been too worried about the death note until now. His mate looked as if she was more than capable of taking him out with a thought at the moment. "Honey, did I tell you I'm sorry lately? I am."

Her lips twitched. "You've mentioned it once or twice today."

"Yes. The alpha just rolls off you in waves," said Blackbeard snidely. "Mississippi, can I speak with you privately?"

"No." Curt crossed his arms over his chest.

Missi ignored his manly show and pushed around in front of him. "How did you get in past the wards? And why are you only in a towel? Where have you been? Why do cursed coins from your treasure keep showing up around Curt with different markings on them? Why did you issue a death note? You told me you didn't practice dark magic anymore."

Blackbeard stared down at Missi and then up at Curt and sneered. "I didn't issue any death note or cursed coins, but I'm very much looking forward to figuring out who did."

"Try not to look so happy," snapped Curt.

"I would but why bother? I've known you five minutes and don't much care for you," returned Blackbeard.

Missi sighed. "Please try to get along."

They nodded.

Blackbeard took a deep breath before speaking. "I'm not sure what happened. All I know was that Flanks was being a pain in my backside again the other night and I was about to tell him where he could stick his suggestion box and property line when a massive amount of magic hit me. I came to face first on the shore and from what I could gather, I'd washed up there. I was missing my clothing. Like what happened when I was cursed into the bottle."

Missi gasped. "Someone cast you out to sea with magic?"

"Not just out to sea, Mississippi," said

Blackbeard. "I think they sent me to one of my sunken treasure ships."

"One? How many do you have?" asked Curt.

Blackbeard ignored him.

"How do you know?" asked Missi.

"Because I came to clutching one of the gold coins that are hidden in the wreckage. The treasure boxes they're in are enchanted, to keep them pristine. Opening the boxes without me there to undo the spell would leave the coins within cursed. The curse doesn't affect me since it's my magic on them, but there is no telling what would happen to whoever ended up with the coins."

Curt lifted a hand. "I started making change earlier."

Blackbeard looked confused.

Curt reached into his pocket and withdrew the coin with the lion head and witch symbol on it.

Blackbeard snatched it out of his hand quickly. "What are you doing with this? How did you get it?"

"Listen, Not-So-Dead-Dude-In-A-

Towel, I didn't ask for that or the hundreds of others that started appearing around me at random all day."

Blackbeard's expression fell. "That would mean you were cursed."

Missi sighed. "I kind of cursed him on top of that too."

Blackbeard laughed.

Curt grunted.

Blackbeard eyed the coin once more. "And did you catch the part where I said *were* cursed?"

"As in past tense?" asked Curt.

Nodding, Blackbeard tossed the coin to him. "Look closer at it."

Curt did and realized there was the smallest of markings on it. He peered at it and then tipped his head. "Is that Old English?"

Blackbeard inclined his head. "It is. Says your freed from the mark of death and ill will. Also says you're joined to a powerful line of magics."

Missi gasped and then threw herself at Curt, hugging him tight. "You're not cursed anymore!"

He wrapped his arms around his wife and savored the feel of her. "Well, at least until you're annoyed with me again."

Blackbeard cleared his throat. "Can we maybe focus here a moment on who cursed you with my magic to start with? It wasn't me. And I sure in the hell didn't vanquish myself."

"Mississippi? Lemon Drop, where are you?"

Curt tensed at the sound of a woman's voice coming from the shop below.

"Mémé Marie-Claire, I'm coming!" yelled Missi, hurrying away from Curt in the direction of the stairs.

Blackbeard caught Curt's arm before he could follow behind Missi. "Break her heart in any way and they'll never recover your body. Am I clear?"

Curt grinned. "Aye, aye, Captain."

Blackbeard groaned and in the next second a large parrot came flying out from the back bedroom. It went right at Blackbeard and landed on the man's bare shoulder. It began to whistle, and it took Curt a second to realize he recognized the song.

"Is your bird whistling a ZZ Top song?" asked Curt.

Blackbeard huffed. "Winston is not my bird. He's your mate's familiar. And yes, he's a fan of classic rock. He apparently thinks you're flashy too since he's whistling 'Sharp Dressed Man.'"

Chapter Twelve

MISSI HURRIED into the magic shop and stopped when she found her grandmother standing next to her father. The two generally avoided being around each other.

Fear raced through her. "Something happened to York, didn't it?"

Her father sighed. "No, darlin'. York is fine. Sig and the rest of them radioed in. They found him. His boat ran into some issues and broke down. They're workin' on fixin' it now. Ought to be back before two shakes of a stick."

She exhaled and then smiled wide.

When she realized her father and

grandmother weren't smiling, she tensed. "What's wrong? Is it about Curt?"

"Kind of," said her grandmother, reaching up and adjusting her hair. It was long, wavy and big. It kept her closer to the Goddess that way. At least that was what she said. She didn't look anywhere near her age—whatever that was. Missi never dared to ask. She did know that her grandmother didn't look a day over fifty. A long chunk of stark white hair went through the crown of her otherwise dark hair. That was really the only sign she had any sort of age creeping up on her and she'd had that as long as Missi could remember.

Marie-Claire stood and smoothed the front of her long, flowing flowered dress. Countless beaded necklaces adorned her neck and matching bracelets filled her wrists, going partway up her arms. She and Missi dressed a lot alike, much to the dismay of Missi's father. He'd never been too fond of the fact his youngest daughter took after his mother-in-law so much.

Missi looked between her father and grandmother. "What's going on? Why are y'all here together? Y'all never go anywhere together. Mémé Marie-Claire, tell me you didn't hex Daddy again. The last time you did it the lights and siren on his squad car wouldn't shut off for nearly three days. And if that wasn't bad enough, every time he opened the trunk, hundreds of frogs leapt out.

Mémé Marie-Claire looked proud of herself. "That was one of my better hexes."

"Marie-Claire," her father said sternly.

"What?" her grandmother asked as if she didn't see the problem. "Admit it. It was a good one."

"Marie-Claire?" asked Blackbeard, appearing in the magic shop with Curt right behind him.

Winston was on Blackbeard's shoulder. He certainly looked every bit the pirate with the bird on his shoulder. Winston had always had a soft spot for the man and Blackbeard humored him.

Missi's father's eyes widened. "Blackbeard, why in tarnation are you missin' your clothes and comin' from my daughter's apartment?"

"It's not what you think," said Curt, a serious look upon his handsome face.

Her father narrowed his gaze on Blackbeard and then glanced from him to her grandmother and back again. "I think you found yourself magically thrust out of the town limits, naked as a jaybird—just like what happened when you got put in that bottle—and figured out your magic and treasure had been tampered with and gone sideways. I'm guessin' the minute you were able, you latched on to the trail of your magic, and found yourself standing in my daughter's apartment, near the cat-shifter."

Curt rubbed his chin. "Never mind. It's exactly what you think. You have got to tell me how you do that."

Her father opened his mouth and then closed it fast, sniffing the air, his eyes swirling to look a lot like an alligator's. It was a sign he was good and mad. He pointed at Curt. "You claimed her! I said you weren't allowed to touch her. Not until she was like eighty or somethin'. I warned you. I told you I'd take you out to the swamps. Boy, have you got any sense up in that Yankee brain of yours? It's like the wheel is spinnin' but the hamster is dead."

Curt's gaze went to the cat toy section that he was near. A lazy smile came to his face.

Mémé laughed and tried to cover it with a cough.

Her father tried to go at Curt only to find Blackbeard stepping in his path and grabbing a hold of him. With both hands on her father, nothing was holding up Blackbeard's towel. It fell to the floor.

Missi gasped in surprise.

She and her grandmother tipped their heads, looks of admiration on their faces, as they stared at the pirate who was wearing only a parrot on his shoulder.

The shop door opened. Jasmine hurried in with Missi's mother and Ms. Cherry. All three women stopped in their tracks, tipped their heads, as well and soaked in the sight of the very naked pirate.

Winston picked that moment to start whistling Rod Stewart's "Do Ya Think I'm Sexy." Her familiar may have been a bully, but he had an uncanny ability to pick a song for the moment.

Her father set his sights on her. "Young lady, control your bird."

"Nonsense," said Mémé Marie-Claire. "He's fine. Very, very fine."

"Mother, are you still talking about the bird?" asked Missi's mom, her gaze moving to Blackbeard. "My goodness, he is very fine indeed."

Her father looked up. "It's a wonder I make it through an entire day without pullin' my hair out."

"Look at it this way, Walden," said Mémé Marie-Claire. "Statistically, you're going to lose your hair anyway. Eventually."

"Mississippi!" shouted Curt, moving around Blackbeard and coming right for her.

Her father turned and when he spotted his wife staring at a naked pirate, he did a double take. "Murielle!"

Blackbeard bent and retrieved his towel slowly, as if standing in front of a room full of women with only a parrot on his shoulder wasn't out of the realm of normal.

He wrapped the towel around himself and all the women sighed.

"Shame to cover that," said Mémé Marie-Claire.

"I agree," said Missi.

Missi's mother laughed. "It is, isn't it? Curt is very attractive. We should ask to see him without his shirt on. Mississippi would know what he looks like under the flashy clothes. Can you sense it in the air? They're mated now."

Curt caught Missi around the waist and drew her against him. His lip found her ear. "Can you not gawk at dead pirate guys, please?"

She snorted. "I'll do my best."

"It's a big ask," said her grandmother.

Blackbeard grumbled. "I prefer the term formally-living."

Her father rubbed his brow, looking tired. "You women are gonna be the death of me."

"We can only hope," said Mémé Marie-Claire.

Her father's jaw set. "Marie-Claire, you need to tell them what you told me."

"Mémé?" asked Missi, her arm snaking around Curt's waist.

Curt kissed her temple and pressed his lips to her ear. "I'd like it known I'm a hunky specimen of man meat. I'll show you later."

"I can hear you, Warrick," warned her father.

Curt gulped. "Sorry, *Dad*."

Her father cringed.

Mémé Marie-Claire clasped her hands. "Before anyone goes getting their panties in a wad, know that this came from a place of love."

"Mother?" asked Missi's mom, concern in her voice. "Frogs aren't going to start magically appearing in the trunk of my husband's squad car again, are they?"

Jasmine and Ms. Cherry moved over to stand near the register, staying quiet.

Mémé Marie-Claire cleared her throat. "I'm not getting any younger and I want to see my grandbabies happy, with families of their own. I want to know the Caillat witch line will continue on and not end because the youngest generation is in no hurry to find their chosen ones. Since their father is in no hurry to get them mated off either, I thought I'd take matters into my own hands."

Missi's stomach sank. She was sure she wasn't going to like whatever it was her grandmother had done. "Mémé, what did you do?"

Mémé Marie-Claire bit her lower lip and then straightened her shoulders. "I might have tapped into some powerful magic to cast a spell to help each of you connect with your mates. Jasmine, I know you're not blood, but you're like a granddaughter to me so I included you."

"Um, thanks," said Jasmine, casting Missi a desperate look.

Missi's mother sighed. "Oh Mother. No. Tell me you didn't."

"I did. I thought I had everything I needed and then I got to thinking about what happened years ago—when I cursed the man I cared for—and I just, well I wasn't paying attention. I got worked up emotionally and my tears mixed into the spell. The spell got away from me. At the same moment there was other power in the air."

Blackbeard gasped. "Flanks and I were drawing on our magics when we were arguing."

Ms. Cherry lifted her hand. "I was usin' magic to help me find the perfect way to get Rockey out of the theater for good. I didn't do it, mind you. I swear. I was only lookin'. I got the list of what I needed and bought it from the shop, but I didn't banish him. Yet. The old-goat is still there, poutin'."

Missi touched her forehead. "You're telling me that four magics combined at once?"

Mémé Marie-Claire nodded. "Yes. And the end result was pandemonium in the magical sense of the word. I think I might have inadvertently cursed each of my grandchildren and their future mates. Since I put a stipulation on the spell about mating, the spell and curses can only be lifted once the true mates' hearts are one."

Missi thought about the strange magic she'd felt when she and Curt had first kissed. She realized then that had been the curse breaking.

Her father grunted. "So my baby nearly got run over and ended up with a cat-shifter because you wanted to be a great-grandmother?"

"Don't sound so excited to have me as part of the family there, Sheriff," said Curt with a wink. "People will start to talk."

Mémé Marie-Claire smiled. "I barely know you and I already like you. The more Walden dislikes you, the closer to my heart you'll be."

"What you're saying is that I'm now you're favorite, right?" asked Curt, nodding to Missi's father. "Since he really does not care for me touching his baby girl."

Missi's mother laughed softly. "Curt, you're going to do just fine as a member of the family now. That is, so long as you don't try to drag his baby far from Hedgewitch Cove."

Curt hugged Missi to him. "Ma'am, I'd never make her leave her home. I'd like to take her to Everlasting to meet all my friends there and maybe help me make arrangements for my businesses up there to be run without me close by. Then I'd like to see to it we build a home here in town and start a family."

"Gonna be hard to do with you not bein' allowed to touch her and all," snapped her father.

Mémé Marie-Claire smiled wide. "Don't be silly, Walden. It's already done."

"What?" asked Missi's father and Curt at the same time.

Blackbeard lifted a hand and his magic raced around the shop, settling on Missi. The pirate grinned. "She's right. It's already done. Congratulations are in order. That is, if you think the flashy guy is a prize."

Curt grunted.

Winston began to whistle ZZ Top, causing Curt to shake his head and shield his eyes with his hand as if he couldn't bear to look anymore.

Missi leaned against her mate and caressed his chest through his shirt. "I do consider him a prize."

Curt moved his hand from his face and locked gazes with her. She went to her tiptoes and planted a chaste kiss on his lips. "I'll have you know I'm not that flashy."

"Uh-huh," she teased. "Sure."

"Yay, another celebration to plan!" shouted Ms. Cherry, tearing up as she did. "I just love a happy ending."

"I'm gonna be a grandpappy?" asked Missi's father.

Her mother went to him and hugged him. "Yes, you are. And don't try to fool anyone. You're happy. You've been wanting this for some time."

"Yes. But Arizona and Georgia were supposed to find their mates first. They're oldest. Not my baby."

Her mother laughed. "Mother's spell may be broken on Curt and Missi, but it's still in effect for the rest of the kids, Jasmine included."

Curt squeezed Missi tight as she soaked in what everyone was saying.

"No," she whispered, unable to believe it.

Curt grinned from ear to ear.

Her eyes widened. "Why do you look so happy?"

He tilted her chin and locked gazes with her. "Because today has been the best day of my life."

She stared at him. "But you were cursed for most of it."

"I know, right? Getting cursed is really the best thing to happen to me. I got a wife and family out of it."

"You're okay with all of this?" she asked.

He bent and kissed her passionately.

Her father cleared his throat.

"Loosen up a little, Walden," said Mémé Marie-Claire.

"I'll loosen up just as soon as you face Petey. He should be back soon enough from helpin' York," said her father.

Mémé Marie-Claire gasped. "On that note, I should be going. Welcome to the family, Curt."

Chapter Thirteen

CURT SAT ON THE DOCK, overlooking the water in a camping chair with his feet propped on a cooler. To his right was Sigmund, Leo and Hugh and to his left was Jake, Petey and Wilber.

"Place kind of grows on you, doesn't it?" asked Sigmund as he sipped his beer, staring out at the water with something close to longing on his face. The half-moon reflected off the water top.

"You ever planning to go home?" asked Curt.

Sigmund's face tightened, and he gripped his beer more. "I don't know that I can. I mean, I know people understand what happened, but I'm not ready to forgive myself right now. I might not ever be."

"So you're thinking of staying down here for good?" asked Curt.

"I honestly don't know what I'm thinking," confessed Sigmund. "I just know I'm not ready to go back to Everlasting just yet. Broke the news to Aunt Jolene early this morning over the phone. I'm guessing she'll be down here before too long, yanking me by my ear back home."

"Of that you can be sure," added Wilber.

"Are you and my aunt dating?" asked Sigmund of the older hunter.

Jake laughed. "Watch out. He gets cranky when you ask about what is and what isn't going on between him and Jolene."

Wilber gave Jake a murderous look before Jake burst into a fit of laughter.

Leo even grinned as he watched Jake. "When beer is added to you, you're all right."

Jake nodded and took a swig from his

beer. "Funny, the more I sit here drinking, the more you grow on me too."

"We're not hugging again," snapped Leo.

"Did you toss the rest of the baked goods that were tainted?" asked Curt of Hugh.

His friend nodded. "Yes. Took me three searches of Petey's room at the inn. I swear he found hiding spaces I couldn't even wrap my mind around."

Petey pointed at him. "You are a fun killer. Your friend murders Shirleys and you murder fun."

"Speaking of Shirley," said Leo, glancing down at Curt. "I think I'll be able to get her all rebuilt for Missi. Her dad keeps a garage full of tools and what not and I think I can get the bike back to like it was before."

"Can you give her streamers?" asked Petey, his eyes wide. "Oh, a bell. I love bikes with bells."

Leo grinned and drank his beer. "Yes. I'll give her both."

"Thank you," said Curt.

Hedgewitch Cove had been home to Curt for all of three days now and he had to admit that it was growing on him. He couldn't be sure, but it seemed as if the entire town had sought he and Missi out to congratulate them. Curt had also lost track of the number of impromptu celebrations that had been organized on the fly over the past few days. All seemed to revolve around Curt and Missi. He was starting to think the townsfolks invented reasons to get together and eat.

Not that he was complaining.

He liked to eat as much as the next alpha male. Even with that, he had to admit his new friends and neighbors had outdone themselves. The small refrigerator at the apartment couldn't handle the sudden influx of casseroles and pies that descended upon them from everyone in town. Petey and Hugh had made a decent dent in them but even the two bottomless pits couldn't seem to keep up. Missi had started to fill the fridge at her sister's restaurant with them.

Hugh groaned as he leaned back in his chair and patted his torso.

Wilber snorted. "Uncomfortable?"

"I watched him eat two entire sweet potato pies before we came down here," said Curt with a laugh. "You should have seen him go at the fried chicken Ms. Cherry brought. I don't know how he's not sick."

"Because he didn't hold his wind in," added Petey who had surprised Curt and brought sweet tea with him to drink in place of whiskey. He stared out at the water, his eyes moist.

Curt hadn't pushed the man even though he knew that Petey had been going out of his way to avoid Marie-Claire. She'd been doing the same, so it wasn't Curt's place to step in. Each one asked about the other often, and it was clear they cared, but neither had taken the first step.

Missi, Virginia, and their mother had other ideas and had been doing their best to get Marie-Claire and Petey in the same location at the same time.

"*He's* coming," said Leo, holding his beer with one hand on his jean-covered thigh as he relaxed in his chair.

Curt stiffened as Blackbeard materialized out of thin air. The man was totally solid, nothing ghost-like about him. He held a bottle of rum in one hand and a folding camping chair in the other.

Curt gave Petey a hard look. "You just had to invite him to boy's night?"

Hugh laughed. "He's all right for a pirate."

Blackbeard grunted. "Thanks. You're all right for a shifter."

"Wait until you bring Penelope down here and she sees him," warned Curt. "When you see your mate drooling over another guy's chest, you change your mind on the guy, real fast."

Hugh seemed to think on it. He sat up straight in his chair. "Never mind. I don't want my mate anywhere around him and his pirate-hot-ness."

Jake chuckled. "Hey, I plan to keep my woman far from him, but I already knew Blackbeard's appeal on women. It's always been that way. I swear he's like the Pied Piper of chicks."

Blackbeard appeared uncomfortable with the topic of discussion as he set his chair next to Leo and took a seat. He glanced at the young hunter. "Heard you were planning to stay on and help Louis with the antique shop and the artifacts now that he's got a spell of chaos on him."

Leo nodded. "Wil thought it would be best."

Wilber cleared his throat. "I thought Warrick was hell-bent on ending the world by way of breaking artifacts. Louis is fast taking the lead. That young man has nearly killed himself and everyone around him a good ten times in the last seventy-two hours."

"Hardly his fault," added Blackbeard. "Marie-Claire's spell is wreaking havoc all throughout that family. York's boat has had how many issues since the curse started?"

Sigmund nodded. "York finally decided to stay on land. Seems like every time he steps foot on his boat something bad happens."

"Missi told me her other brother and sister are suffering the effects of it too," added Curt.

"Oh, I'm sure," said Wilber. "Marie-Claire's line of witches is darn powerful."

Petey rubbed his wiry chin. "That they are."

"You made out though with the curse," said Blackbeard to Curt. "A new wife. A little one on the way. Seems like you did well for yourself considering."

Curt didn't want to like the guy who seemed to turn every female's head, but he had to admit that like Hedgewitch Cove, the pirate was growing on him. "I did. Never thought I'd be happy I got cursed."

"Who is that?" asked Leo, pointing down the dock.

A lone figure approached. He had on a dark surrey hat and matching rainslicker, even though it wasn't raining. That wasn't all the man had on. No. He was also wearing a sign that had This is the End painted across it. He had a megaphone in his hand. Lifting it, he shouted, "Beware. The end comes. It's upon us."

Blackbeard groaned. "Arnold, what did I tell you?"

The man stopped and hung his head.

"That I'm not the bringer of the apocalypse or harbinger of doom, and I'm not allowed to walk around town announcing anything about the world ending."

Apocalypse Arnold?

Curt and Hugh shared a look before they glanced down at Petey.

"Turns out, Petey really did once know everyone," said Curt with a snort.

"You ready to head out in the morning?" asked Hugh of Petey.

The older man continued to stare out at the water. "I think I might stay on down here for a while longer myself. Figure Warrick, Bails, and Leo need someone to keep an eye on them all."

Wilber stood and folded his chair. "I think that sounds like a wonderful idea, Petey. I'm heading back to Luc's and calling it a night. I'm also planning to book a flight home. Hugh, Jake, want me to do the same for the two of you so you don't have to drive all the way back in Sunshine?"

Hugh and Jake stood fast, both shouting "yes" at the same time.

Curt laughed. He'd miss them all when

they left but he knew they'd continue to see one another. This was hardly the end for them, but it was a new beginning for Curt.

THE END

Note to readers: Want to read Hugh's story? Buy **Once Hunted, Twice Shy** today! Want to read Jake's story? Buy **Total Eclipse of the Hunt** today!

Excerpt: Once Hunted, Twice Shy

The following material is free of charge. It will never affect the price of your book.

Once Hunted, Twice Shy by Mandy M. Roth

Welcome to Everlasting, Maine, where there's no such thing as normal.

WOLF SHIFTER HUGH LUPINE simply wants to make it through the month and win the bet he has with his best friend. He's not looking to date anyone, or to solve a murder, but when a breath taking beauty runs him over (literally) he's left no choice but to take notice of the quirky, sassy newcomer. She'd be perfect if it wasn't for the fact she's the granddaughter of the local supernatural hunter. Even if he can set aside his feelings about her family, Penelope is his complete opposite in all ways.

Penelope Messing wanted to get away from the harsh reminder that her boyfriend of two years dumped her. Several pints of ice cream and one plane ticket to Maine later, she's ready to forget her troubles. At least for a bit. When she arrives in the sleepy little fishing town of Everlasting, for a surprise visit with her grandfather, she soon learns that outrunning one problem can lead to a whole mess of others. She finds herself the prime suspect in a double homicide. She doesn't even kill spiders, let alone people, but local law enforcement has their eyes on her.

The secrets of Everlasting come to light and Penelope has to not only accept that things that go bump in the night are real, but apparently, she's destined for a man who sprouts fur and has a bizarre obsession with fish sticks. Can they clear Penelope's name and set aside their differences to find true love?

EXCERPT FROM ONCE HUNTED, Twice Shy

Penelope Messing tapped her cell phone, wondering what was happening to her GPS. It had suddenly lost its mind. She sat in her rental car, pulled off to the side of a narrow road near a large lighthouse. The navigation system had been fine one second and had tried to route her into the ocean the next. The voice, which was set to a female one, had been rather insistent that she continue onward. The screen with the map displayed had very clearly shown nothing but water, but that didn't seem to matter.

The darn thing had unrelentingly told her that her destination was ahead. It even had a flag graphic shown on the display with nothing but blue surrounding it. Unless her grandfather had taken to living in a submarine and no longer resided behind his shop, in the center of town, the directions the system was giving her were faulty.

Even worse, the rental car came equipped with navigation in the dash, and it too seemed to think she needed to be in the ocean. Having two different navigation systems want to drown her was unnerving to say the least.

She pulled up the address on her phone that she'd keyed in at the airport to be sure she'd not made an error. She hadn't. This one-lane road did not look like Main Street to her. If it was, the town of Everlasting had sure downsized since she'd last been there, not that it had been a sprawling metropolis or anything before.

Prior to finding the lighthouse, all that had surrounded Penelope had been trees on both sides of the road, leaving barely any shoulder to the road at all. The dense woods had gone on for what felt like an eternity. She'd been excited when she found a structure at the end of the narrowing road. As she glanced at the huge lighthouse, she wasn't so sure it was her saving grace after all. With the heavy rains, winds and thunder booming, the lighthouse looked less like a welcoming beacon and more like an ominous warning.

If she thought she'd be able to find her way back to the airport, and to the city, she'd have already turned around and made a go for it. At least there she'd be able to find a hotel room for the night and wait out the weather. As it stood, she was committed and starting to feel as if she'd driven to the town time forgot.

Just then, lightning slashed the sky behind the lighthouse, causing Penelope to jolt upright in the car. She hit her knee on the steering wheel and winced. "Son of a bumblebee, that hurt."

On the verge of tears, she rubbed her knee, rethinking her life choices in a big way. Had she just stayed in Chicago, she wouldn't currently be lost and parked near the spooky lighthouse. Had she just turned Craig down two years ago when he'd insisted they go to dinner together, she wouldn't have a broken heart.

Frustration gnawed at her, picking away at her inner defenses like a festering wound.

Everything had led her to this point, and second-guessing it all was getting her nowhere fast.

She'd wanted to get away from the city, away from her life there, away from her ex and his newly announced bride-to-be, and spend time with her grandfather. It should have been easy.

So far, the flight in had been delayed several hours due to a broken windshield wiper that wouldn't go down. Once they'd finally gotten on their way, turbulence had rocked the plane nonstop. Upon landing, she'd found out they'd lost her checked luggage, but the airlines were quick to let her know that should they locate her bags, they'd have them delivered to where she was staying. And what should have been an easy drive to Everlasting was proving to be anything but.

"You are not going to die by the creepy-looking lighthouse, surrounded by even creepier woods and an ocean that looks like it wants to swallow you whole."

Now if she only believed herself, all would be well.

I'm a goner.

As she tapped her phone, she caught the slightest of movements out of the corner of her eye. Looking up, she spotted a man in the window of the lighthouse. Maybe the lighthouse wasn't so creepy after all. Especially if she could get some help there.

Hope welled, and she considered getting out to ask for directions. If he lived here, he surely knew his way around.

That thought died the moment the man backed up from the window, and she got a good look at what he was wearing, or rather what he *wasn't* wearing—pants.

He was in a sports jacket and a pair of plaid boxers.

Nothing else.

"Oh my stars," she breathed as her eyes widened. She let off the brakes momentarily, and the car crept forward, toward the cliff side. She hit the brakes and put the car in park, needing to get her bearings and then put some distance between herself and the older gentleman wearing boxers. It was that or drive off the cliff to her death because the sight of him there was like a train wreck—something she couldn't look away from.

A series of sneezes came over her, and she held tight to the wheel, thankful she had pulled the car to a stop. Had she not, the GPS might have very well gotten its way and had her swimming with the fishes. Every bad mafia pun she could think of rolled through her head, causing a nervous laugh to escape her. She sneezed more, so hard that she nearly hit her forehead on the steering wheel.

Penelope snatched her purse from the passenger seat and took out a pack of tissues. She touched her nose with one, wondering what had come over her. Normally, she only sneezed in such a manner when she was around cats. She had a strong allergy to them and therefore did her best to avoid them whenever possible. If she didn't, she'd end up with puffy eyes and a runny nose that would last for days. Once she'd stayed at a friend's house who had two cats and her eyes had swollen completely shut. That had lasted for nearly a week and had required a shot to help clear up.

Thankfully, she had no issues with dogs and had a major soft spot for them. She'd have gotten one of her own if her lifestyle permitted it. As it was, she worked so many hours that it would have been unfair to any animal. In the meantime, she donated to animal shelters and rescue groups to help sate her longing for a furry friend. Whenever she could, she also volunteered, being sure to point out she couldn't help with any cats.

Currently, there were no cats to be seen. She sneezed more, her body begging to differ with her.

She returned the tissue pack to her purse and set her purse back on the passenger seat of the vehicle, near her carry-on bag. Her carry-on held her laptop, charging cords, and a few personal items. Having to travel a great deal for the auction house, Penelope had learned to keep a change of clothes in whatever carry-on bag she took on a flight. She was relieved she'd had the forethought to do so now, or she'd be stuck in what she was wearing indefinitely.

She adjusted her sweater that had a puppy knitted on the front of it. Her sense of fashion had always been quite different from that of other women her age, but she didn't care. At twenty-six, she wore what made her smile, and the sweater had given her the warm fuzzies when she'd spotted it in a storefront window. The leggings that she wore with it had small fire hydrants on them and paired perfectly with the sweater. At five feet nine inches, she'd had to hunt around the internet for a pair that would fit her long legs, but she'd managed to find some.

Craig, her boyfriend of the last two years, and the man who had broken her heart into a million pieces, had hated the way she dressed when she wasn't at work. He'd mocked it every chance he'd gotten and had refused more than once to be seen in public with her until she'd changed her clothes. He also greatly disliked her sayings and refusal to say curse words. She'd always found a foul mouth to be a waste of energy. Besides, it was more fun to think of creative alternatives to words that shouldn't be said in polite company.

Craig had never agreed.

Looking back, she realized they'd never really had much in common. She loved old things, antiques of any kind, and architecture. He liked money and knocking down old buildings to make way for new ones.

They'd met while she was working at the auction house and she'd been in her professional attire. He'd come into the auction house with a friend of his who had items up for bid, and then he'd insisted she have dinner with him. He'd seemed sweet and charming, but it had all been for show. He was on the hunt for the proper wife to drag around to social functions, and she wasn't it. She wanted nothing to do with high society. She'd given him two years of her life, thinking the entire time that the relationship was going somewhere. That it had a future.

How foolish she'd been.

He'd broken up with her in an expensive restaurant, making quite the scene about how clumsy she was, how her sense of fashion was laughable and how she was book smart but would never be good wife material. He was also stuck on her lack of wanting to advance further in her career. She was content with what she did and didn't want to push onward. She made good money, more than she needed to live a modest lifestyle, and she liked the people she worked with. There was no reason to want more. Craig had never understood that.

Three days ago, she'd opened the newspaper to find his photo there in the engagement section with a beautiful woman smiling next to him. Within a month of their breakup, he'd not only moved on, he'd also found that cookie-cutter trophy wife he'd been so desperate for. He was living his dream, and she was in the middle of a nightmare. She'd thought she'd been in love with Craig, and that he'd felt the same for her. A small part of her had even hoped their breakup was temporary. Clearly, it wasn't. The sting of it all was still fresh enough to make her tear up.

She blinked away the pending tears.

She'd shed enough of them over the man.

Within minutes of seeing the announcement in the paper, Penelope had finished off an entire apple pie and cried for several hours before getting online and booking a flight to Everlasting. So far, her last-minute trip was proving to be anything but relaxing.

"It can only get better from here, right?"

Glancing back up at the lighthouse, Penelope assumed she'd see the man in the plaid boxers once more. She didn't. He was gone from the window, and there was no light whatsoever in the lighthouse any longer. As much as she needed a helping hand with directions, she didn't want to go up to the lighthouse and ask.

She had a great-uncle who liked to walk around in his boxers as well when she was younger, and the image was still seared into her brain. At least the man in the lighthouse had gone with a nice sports jacket rather than a holey white undershirt that her great-uncle had been partial to.

Conjuring a mental image of her great-uncle, she shuddered, did a four-point turn, and drove the rental car back down the narrow road, hoping to spot a landmark or sign that would jog her memory. It had been a long time since she'd been in Everlasting. The sleepy little fishing village had apparently grown in size, at least from what she'd read on the internet.

Truth be told, she'd never thought she'd return. Her last memory of the area was of attending her parents' funeral. She'd walked silently behind the black vehicles that had held her mother's and father's coffins, her hand in her grandpa Wil's, her heart broken beyond repair. It had all seemed so confusing to her back then, like a whirl, everything happening so fast.

Her entire world had changed on a dime, and nothing had been the same. She'd been six years old then. Twenty years had passed, but it felt like yesterday. The raw emotions of it all were there, just below the surface, wanting to come out. She held tight to them, mentally reminding herself that she was no longer six years old.

She was a grown woman.

Still, the sting of it was there, floating on her memories of the time. Within hours of laying her parents to rest, she'd been whisked away from the town by her mother's parents to be raised far from Everlasting—far from Wilber Messing, her grandfather. She'd found herself in a small town in Mississippi until she'd gone off to college.

She had fond childhood memories of Grandpa Wil. He'd been attentive and caring when she was a child, always telling her one fantastical tale after another. He never ran out of interesting stories about mythical creatures and monsters that were purportedly real. He'd tell of times of old when he and his ancestors supposedly hunted these made-up creatures. He'd had a way about him that was whimsical, and that made her smile. He'd often taken her hiking in the woods on the edge of town, teaching her to track wild animals and to fish. And he'd always made her feel safe and loved.

She'd been devastated when her parents had died and even more distraught when she'd been taken far from Grandpa Wil.

Her mother's parents had felt he was a bad influence and unfit to raise a small child on his own. They'd forbid her from visiting him or contacting him while she was growing up. Once she was away from their clutches, she'd reached out to him, hoping he'd want to see her once more.

He'd come right away to visit her at her university and had made trips across the country to spend time with her every year since, even after she'd gotten her master's degree and started her job in marketing. But not this year.

That was part of the reason why she'd decided to fly in and surprise him. The other part had been because of her ex-boyfriend and the rather harsh reminder she wasn't wife material in the morning paper. She'd cashed in all her unused vacation time, and she'd left the hustle and bustle of Chicago for the sleepy seaside fishing town of Everlasting.

The more she struggled to find anything that looked familiar, the more she thought she should have called first and given him a heads-up. She came to a spot in the road

Don't Stop Bewitching

where she had to make a choice, left or right. She went with right and soon found herself driving down a narrow road, on a cliff side that overlooked the ocean. The storm was still going strong, so Penelope went slow, wanting to arrive in Everlasting safe, not be fished out of the bottom of the ocean by a search-and-rescue dive team.

She clutched the wheel tighter, white-knuckling her drive, as she wondered if Everlasting even had a search-and-rescue team at all. They weren't exactly a large town.

When the rain reached a rate that made it impossible for the rental car's wipers to keep up, she pulled the car to the side of the road once more, put the hazard lights on, and parked. She'd wait it out before she tried to push onward. There was no sense in risking life and limb to get there sooner. Check-in at the bed-and-breakfast she was staying at wasn't until later in the day, so she had plenty of time yet.

She wasn't sure how long she sat there before a set of yellow flashing lights came up from behind her. The lights were too bright to see what type of vehicle was there, but it was evident it was a sizeable one. Vaguely, Penelope made out a shadowy figure making its way toward her car.

She tensed, having seen one too many horror movies in her lifetime. As the figure drew closer, fear raced up Penelope's spine. The person was wearing rain gear from head to toe and walking slowly, dragging one leg slightly. Lightning rent the sky behind the figure, making them look even more ominous.

Oh boy, she thought.

Paralyzed by fear, she sat perfectly still, positive the newcomer would succeed where the GPS had failed and actually kill her. She'd end up a statistic. A footnote in a local paper.

Coming to her senses, Penelope made sure the car locks were engaged and then looked around for anything that could be used as a weapon. Much to her dismay, the only object that might work was a ballpoint pen. Still, she clutched it for dear life, her heart pounding madly.

There was a hard rap on the window,

and Penelope yelped, suddenly wishing she'd taken her chances with the man in boxers. She turned her head, unsure what she'd find, but positive it would be something horror-film worthy.

Much to her surprise, she found a woman who looked to be in her mid-sixties there, tapping lightly on the driver-side window, a huge, nonthreatening smile on her face.

Penelope sighed with relief, rolling down the window.

The woman beamed. "Lost?"

"And then some," replied Penelope, releasing her death grip on the ballpoint pen.

"Where you headed?" asked the woman, a Maine accent evident.

"Everlasting," replied Penelope, ignoring the rain that was coming in at her from the open window.

The woman laughed. "Well, child, you're in luck. You're *in* Everlasting. There was a sign down the road there. Couldn't have missed it."

Penelope's face reddened. She'd more

than missed the sign. "Really? My GPS told me I had another twenty minutes. Right before it tried to drive me off a cliff into the ocean."

The woman waved a hand flippantly. "Those don't work so well around these parts. Follow my truck, and I'll get you off this stretch of road and closer to the heart of town. Tonight isn't a night for wandering."

"Thank you." Penelope barely got the words out before the woman was headed back to her truck.

They couldn't drive fast with the rain, but it didn't take long before they encountered something that looked like civilization. A small roadside fuel and service station was there, along with a hotel and tiny restaurant. Every parking space in the hotel lot was filled. Penelope wouldn't have thought of Everlasting as a tourist destination, but she was starting to wonder.

CLICK TO BUY ONCE HUNTED, Twice Shy

About the Author

Dear Reader

Did you enjoy this title and want to know more about Mandy M. Roth, her pen names and all the titles she has available for purchase (over 100)?

About Mandy:

New York Times & *USA TODAY* Bestselling Author Mandy M. Roth loves 80s music and movies and wishes leg warmers would come back into fashion. She also thinks the movie The Breakfast Club should be mandatory viewing for...okay, everyone. When she's not dancing around her office to the sounds of the 80s or writing books, she can be found designing book covers for New York publishers, small presses, and indie authors.

Learn More:

To learn more about Mandy and her pen names, please visit www.Mandy-Roth.com

For latest news about Mandy's newest releases and sales subscribe to her newsletter: Sign Up For Mandy's Newsletter

Want to see all Mandy's books? Click here.

Printable PDF list of all Mandy's titles: Click here.

To join Mandy's Facebook Reader Group: The Roth Heads.

Review this title:

Please consider leaving an honest review on the vendor site in which you purchased this title. Reviews help to spread the word and boost overall sales. This means more books in the series you love.

Thank you!

- facebook.com/AuthorMandyRoth
- twitter.com/mandymroth
- instagram.com/mandymroth
- goodreads.com/mandymroth
- pinterest.com/mandymroth
- bookbub.com/authors/mandy-m-roth
- youtube.com/mandyroth
- amazon.com/author/mandyroth